The Glory Trail

RAY HOGAN

DOUBLEDAY & COMPANY, INC.

GARDEN CITY, NEW YORK 1978

All the characters in this book
are fictional, and any resemblance to
actual persons, living or dead,
is purely coincidental.

Library of Congress Cataloging in Publication Data
Hogan, Ray, 1908–
The Glory Trail
ISBN: 0-385-14280-3
Library of Congress Catalog Card Number: 77-26526

POR LA—

tercero distrito terror, con amor,
desde el cuarto distrito destello

The
Glory Trail

❋1❋

Dazed, Luther Pike watched Deputy Sheriff Pete Peabody ride off toward town. It was late afternoon and the hands he'd been working with at cleaning out the south spring—Arnie Payne, Windy Jackson and his bunkie of many years, Percy Gilmore—had just finished the chore and were getting ready to head back to the ranch.

Equally dazed and thoroughly surprised, they, too, were following the lawman with their eyes as they stood beside their horses, and then as Peabody's figure diminished, they turned their attention to Luther.

"That for sure what you're aiming to do?" Percy asked, a note of resentment in his tone.

Luther nodded. A tall, lean man in his late twenties, with scraggy brown hair and deep set, dark eyes, he had spent his life working first on the family farm as a boy, and then after he'd grown large enough to run away, punching cattle for various ranchers in Texas, New Mexico and Arizona.

Now, standing rigid in the hot June sunlight, battered, high-crowned hat pushed to the back of his head, dust from the day's labor laying a gray film on his faded checked shirt, red bandanna, colorless, worn pants, scarred leather vest and run-down boots, exultation was coursing through him as he visualized the future. At last he was to realize his ambition!

"Just what I been wanting to do forever!" he said in a tense, disbelieving voice.

Percy swore, and stepping away from his horse, squatted in the shade of a nearby mesquite. As if on signal, Windy and Arnie followed and dropped to their haunches. Luther did not move, however, but, as if transfixed, continued to watch Deputy Peabody, now little more than a blur in the heat-hazed distance.

"Well, dang it!" Percy said explosively, "you ain't never mentioned nothing about being no lawman to me!"

Arnie Payne took his jew's-harp from a pocket and began to play a tune of unrecognizable derivation. Luther listened briefly, turned to Gilmore, shrugged.

"Now, I don't have to tell you everything, Percy! We ain't married, you know."

"No, we sure ain't, but I figured we was better friends than that. When'd you tell the sheriff you was wanting to be a deputy?"

Again Luther was caught up with the tune Arnie was twanging out of his harp. He just couldn't seem to place it, and that was unusual for he generally was the only one in the crowd who could tell what Payne was playing.

"Been six months or so," he said.

"Six months!" Percy shouted, "and you never said a thing to me about it? A fine friend you turned out to be."

Windy, by-passing one of his usual stories, which always had a bearing on whatever subject was under discussion, shifted, spat, brushed at the sweat on his round, freckled face. He was much older than Luther and the others, was almost bald and hardly ever got around to using his razor.

"Man won't usually talk much about his own private glory trail," he said. "I reckon that's how it's been with Luther."

"For certain," Luther murmured, glancing once more toward Peabody. The deputy had disappeared entirely from view. "Been hoping for this chance a long time—"

"Six months ain't long," Percy cut in acidly.

"That's how long it's been since I talked to the sheriff—been wanting to wear a star, get myself started on the road to fame and fortune ever since I was big enough to think about it. I aim to make myself a real good deputy, catch myself a bunch of outlaws and collect them big rewards and get a big name like Bat Masterson and Wyatt Earp, and fellows like them, and be somebody important—maybe even a United States Marshal, someday."

Percy swore again. "Danged if you don't beat all! You never let on you was fed up with punching cows—never once said nothing!"

"Don't take much to get fed up with cowpunching," Luther said, mopping at his brow with the back of a hand. "Sure ain't nothing to pulling cockleburs out of a horse's tail, or cutting and tarring bulls and branding calves—and cleaning out a waterhole, and the like. Gets mighty tiresome."

"It don't for me," Percy declared stubbornly.

About the same age as Luther, he was blond, florid, blue-eyed and husky. They had been acquainted for years, and while Luther found Percy's whining and constant complaining a bit wearing at times, he considered him his best and closest friend.

He reckoned he should have expected Percy to kick up a fuss—and he had intended to tell him about talking things over with Sheriff Hollingshead first chance he got— but somehow he'd never got around to it. Anyway, there wasn't any sense in Percy carrying on like he was. Hell, he wasn't going to the moon—just to Linksburg which wasn't but a two-hour ride from the ranch where they all worked.

There was no reason why they still couldn't get together on weekends and shoot pool at Barnett's Pool Parlor, and hoist a few beers at the Hog's Eye Saloon, and do a few twirls with the girls there when they got to feeling right good.

Arnie Payne forsook the jew's-harp. "You tell Mr. Hockmeyer you was aiming to quit?" he asked.

"Nope, sure haven't—never told nobody nothing," Luther replied, nodding at Percy to show him that he hadn't been slighted. "Just ain't been time. I'll be obliged if one of you'll tell him for me—explain how the sheriff was wanting me right off. I'll drop by and pick up my wages, whatever I got coming, first chance I get."

"If you ain't been shot deader'n a doornail," Percy said sourly, as Arnie Payne resumed his musical efforts.

Luther grinned, wagged his head. "Oh, I expect being a lawman ain't all that dangerous. Man just has to watch his hind side. Anyways, a lot of the job's serving papers and investigating stealings, things like that."

"Ain't how that deputy sounded. Said you was to report to the sheriff right away—something about a real important job."

"Prob'ly's got something to do with them rustlers they been trying in court," Windy suggested.

"Prob'ly," Luther agreed, feeling a surge of importance. "I'd best be riding in and seeing just what it is the sheriff's wanting me to do."

He doubted, however, that it had anything to do with the rustlers, whoever they were. Lawmen were called upon to discharge many exciting tasks—like riding shotgun on a big shipment of gold, or being bodyguard to some high-up official like a visiting senator—or even the President. And he could be called on to—

"I just can't see you being a lawman," Percy said. "Why, you can't hardly hit the side of a barn with that old hogleg you're carrying! I'll bet you ain't fired it in over a year."

Luther reached down, drew his pistol, an elderly cap-and-ball-converted forty-four. It was rusting slightly and the butt was plenty scarred from driving nails and being used as a hammer for other purposes, but it was still a trustworthy weapon.

"Well, I don't know about that," he drawled, and quick snapped a shot at a stump at the edge of the spring. The bullet plunked solidly into the wood, sent up a shower of splinters and dust.

Everybody, including the horses, jumped. Luther grinned. "Now, that ain't so bad, is it?"

Percy spat derisively. "You been practicing," he said accusingly, "or it plain was a accident."

"Nope, no such a thing," Luther stated, temper beginning to lift. Percy sure could grate on a man sometimes, and he needed taking down a notch—but Luther reckoned he'd not risk a second shot at the stump just to prove his point.

"Some folks just has natural ability," Windy Jackson observed. "Expect that's how it is with Luther."

Luther smiled self-consciously and shrugged. "I ain't claiming to be no handy-andy with a shooting iron, but I expect I can get by." He paused, listened for a moment to the new tune Arnie was working on, and then continued. "Aim to outfit myself with a new gun and holster soon as I get strung out, anyway. Needing some new duds, too. These I'm wearing sure ain't fit for a lawman."

"No, they ain't—for a fact," Windy said, frankly, biting off a chew of tobacco. "Once knew a marshal—was up Dakota way. I'll tell you he was the niftiest fellow I've ever seen! Wore black cord pants, and one of them shiny, sateen shirts—was black, too, with pearl buttons. Had a leather vest, the real soft kind, and there was a big gold watch chain looping across his belly from the bottom pockets.

"Was wearing a real fine pair of Hyer boots, all fancied up with yellow stitching—curlicues and circles and diamonds—things like that. Then to make hisself look real classy, he had a big white Texas hat on his head—one of them with a high crown and real wide brim—"

"Expect he was wearing two pistols and crossed belts," Percy Gilmore cut in.

Windy frowned, annoyed, shifted his cud. "Yeh, I guess he was. How'd you know?"

Percy's shoulders stirred. "The fancy dressers always do. He find a place to wear a star in all that foofaraw?"

"Yes, sir, right up where it belonged," Windy said, grumpily. "He was a might impressing looking man."

"Might just fix myself up with an outfit like that some-day," Luther said, doing a bit of fantasizing, and enjoying it. "First big reward I collect I'll do me some thinking and looking around about it."

He glanced at the sun. It was swinging low, time he was heading for town and reporting to Sheriff Hollings-head. Deputy Peabody had said the lawman was wait-ing, and standing around jawing like he was could be holding up something real important. Wheeling, he crossed to Windy Jackson and extended his arm.

"*Adios, amigo,* sure has been nice working with you."

Jackson rose, turned his head aside and relieved him-self of a mouthful of brown juice, and clasping Luther's fingers in his own, nodded.

"Same here, partner. You take care."

"Aim to," Luther assured him, and held out his hand to Arnie. "So long. I'm going to miss that whang-doodle playing of yours."

Payne, also coming to his feet, grinned, said, "Drop around anytime—I'll be plumb happy to play you a tune. . . . Luck."

"Obliged, and same to you," Luther said and came full about to face Percy. "Me getting to be a lawman ain't no cause for us to quit playing pool Saturday nights—"

"The hell it ain't!" Gilmore snapped peevishly. "You won't have no time for nothing 'cept being a deputy a'running around the country arresting folks and collecting them big rewards and the like. You're plain going to have to forget about me and the rest of the boys."

"That's pure foolishness, and you know it. Me being a lawman won't make one whit difference," Luther declared, and offered his hand. "I'm mighty sorry you're taking my good luck this way, Percy. You going to shake or not?"

Gilmore's jaw tightened, and then he shrugged. "Reckon I am," he said, and taking Luther's fingers into his own, squeezed firmly. "You right sure you know what you're a'doing? I don't figure you're cut out to be a lawman."

"I'm sure," Luther answered without hesitation, pulling away and moving to his horse. Going to the saddle he looked down at his friends and said, "Be seeing you boys," and then, as an afterthought, added, "I'll be obliged if one of you'll do the explaining to Mr. Hockmeyer for me—tell him what I said."

"I'll do it," Percy snapped, and abruptly turning his back, marched rigidly to his mount. Apparently he still felt hurt by what he considered a slight on the part of Luther. "You just go right ahead being a big-time lawman. The rest of us'll get along all right."

Luther watched the three men pull away. "So long," he murmured, and then raking his horse with his spurs, he cut about and headed for town. There was a tightness in his throat, but he reckoned that was natural. A fellow just couldn't stay in the same rut all his life—friends or not. He owed it to himself to try and do better.

⚒ 2 ⚒

Being the county seat, Linksburg was a town of fair size insofar as settlements in that part of the territory were concerned. It boasted not only of a Main Street but two that paralleled it and one that intersected. Its population, growing steadily it was said, had climbed to nine hundred and seventy, and it was very likely the magic figure of one thousand would be reached by the end of the year.

Such was all lost on Luther since he was not given much to looking into incidental information. His interest and knowledge of the settlement consisted mostly of a working acquaintance of Alamo Avenue, the cross street. There could be found Barnett's Pool Parlor and the Hog's Eye Saloon which offered gambling, meals, girls, dancing, and even rooms for those who, after a night's extensive and exhausting hilarity, felt the need to recuperate before returning to work-a-day life.

Those two mentioned establishments were favored exclusively by Luther and his friends from the ranch, who, like him, had never troubled to learn much else about Linksburg. Now, in the last of the sun's light, as he rode down Main, Luther reckoned he'd best take a bit more notice of the town.

Turner Bros. Family Store . . . The Emporium, which

appeared to handle everything from baby shoes to farm wagons . . . Marcie's Ladies & Children Shop . . . the White Elephant Saloon, a large imposing place in front of which stood several well-dressed men . . . the Drovers' Hotel . . . Barnum's Restaurant, Home-style Cooking . . . the Crown Livery Stable, and two dozen or more additional structures that housed various offices and enterprises.

The residential area lay to the west and east of the town, and Luther could see a scatter of ordinary houses with a larger two- or three-story edifice rising among them at irregular intervals.

Luther whistled softly. Linksburg was quite a town! A lot of buildings—a lot of folks moving about going about their business, he supposed. But he reckoned he'd best start getting used to such if he aimed to become an important lawman. This was the kind of big city he'd be living in, and these were the sort of people he'd be hobnobbing with.

What's more, if all went well, he'd probably end up in Capitol City or some other really big place like it, and he for sure had to know how to act, not let on that he'd never been anything more than a cowhand wet-nursing dogies before he got famous.

Unconsciously Luther drew himself up, sat a bit straighter on his saddle. This was the beginning, the realization of his dream, and he for sure was going to do things right—starting then. His one regret, at the moment, was that he'd not had time to fix himself up with some better clothes so's he'd look like a lawman. But maybe folks wouldn't pay too much attention to him now, looking as he did, like any ordinary cowhand. There was considerable traffic along the street; chances were he wasn't being noticed much.

But that fact took the edge off his more or less triumphant journey down Main Street, and finally pulling his hat lower over his sun- and wind-burned face, he continued along its length until locating the building that housed the jail and sheriff's office, where he angled in to it.

Pulling up at the rack, standing empty in the afternoon heat, Luther halted and swung off the saddle. Wrapping the bay's reins around the crossbar, he paused for a moment as if to gather himself, and then stepping up to the screen door of the lawman's quarters, opened it and entered.

Three men were present: Deputy Peabody who stared at him with his flat, expressionless eyes as if seeing a stranger; Tom Hollingshead, the sheriff—a large, portly man with the smooth look of a successful politician—and a second deputy unknown to Luther.

Drawing up in the center of the stuffy little office, he nodded and grinned at Hollingshead. "Howdy. I'm Luther Pike. You sent the deputy out to fetch me."

The sheriff bobbed crisply, got up from behind his littered desk and shook hands. Back in the jail part of the building several prisoners were singing discordantly while a lone drummer improvised by beating time on the bars of his cell with an object of some sort.

"Glad you came right in," Hollingshead boomed, jerking a thumb at Peabody. "You know Pete there. Maybe you don't know Herb Slocum. He's my chief deputy."

Slocum, a tall, square-jawed man somewhere in his forties, and dressed all in gray except for black stovepipe boots, smiled in friendly fashion and extended his hand.

"Pleased to know you, Pike," he said and stepped back.

Luther could feel all three men giving him the once-over, no doubt wondering why he'd show up for an important job in clothes that looked as if he'd been wallowing in the dirt with a grizzly.

"Never had no time to fix myself up," he said, feeling he'd best explain. "Deputy Peabody said you wanted me to come right in—and that's just what I done."

Hollingshead shrugged. "Don't fret about it. Can get yourself some new clothes later when there's time. Expect all the stores are closed by now, anyway . . . You leaving right away, Pete?"

"Guess I am—seeing as how he's here," Peabody replied, and turning on a heel, moved toward the door. Pushing it open he said, "So long," and stepped out onto the walk.

Hollingshead swung his attention to Slocum, a frown of annoyance pulling at his broad face. "Go shut them damn drunks up," he directed, and motioning for Luther to take a chair, he settled down behind his desk.

"Expect you've heard about the trial that's been going on here," he began, watching Deputy Slocum depart through a doorway that apparently led to the cells in the rear of the building.

Luther rubbed at his jaw reflectively. "Well, I ain't had much time for reading or getting around lately, being busy—"

"Sure, I understand," the lawman said. "Fact is we've

just wound up trying some rustlers. Jury found them all guilty. Judge sentenced three of them to hang. Fourth one's going to the pen at Capitol City to serve a life sentence."

"Just somehow never heard about it," Luther said.

"Was only over yesterday so it's not likely you would have. Finished just when Peabody hit me between the eyes with wanting to quit. Left me short-handed and in a bad fix 'til I remembered your dropping by that time and saying you'd like to go to work as a deputy first opening that came along."

"I sure been looking forward to the chance—"

"Well, it's come and you've got it. Peabody's gone and you're taking his place as second deputy. Now, first job you'll handle is an important one—more important, in fact, than I ought to be turning over to a new man, specially one without any lawing experience. But I've got no choice, and anyway, I figure you're level-headed and got common sense enough to handle it."

"I sure aim to do my best," Luther said, earnestly.

"I know that . . . I ought to handle the job myself, but I've still got to be around for court. There's a couple more trials coming up and I have to be here. Can't use Slocum, either. He's got to make a trip down into Mexico, do some negotiating with one of the generals for a couple of outlaws we want bad. He'll be riding out tonight and hoping to get there before that general changes his mind. Guess that gives you an idea why all the big rush."

The lawman paused, glancing to the doorway as a passerby drew open the screen, thrust his head inside and said, "Evening, Tom. How's the sheriff business?"

Hollingshead smiled patiently, replied, "Fine, Ollie, just fine!"

Slocum had stilled the songbirds and their accompanist, and the only sounds audible were those rising in the street. Luther shifted on his chair. The heat in the office was intense, and reaching up, he brushed at the sweat on his forehead and looked directly at the lawman.

"I reckon what you're getting at is that I'm to take the prisoner to Capitol City."

Hollingshead bobbed. "Exactly what I'm doing. As I said it's an important matter and maybe I'm unfair, unloading it on your shoulders first crack out of the box, but you applied for a job as a deputy so you—"

"Yes, sir, I asked, and I ain't sorry because you're trusting me with a big job. Can figure on me doing it because I aim to prove to you that I'm a top man. When do you want me to head out?"

"Everything's all arranged. You'll be leaving early in the morning."

"That's fine. Horse of mine can use a night's rest. He's been working pretty hard and—"

"You won't be going by horseback—you'll take the stage."

Surprise crossed Luther's face. "That so? I sort of figured to be riding my horse."

Hollingshead mopped at his neck with a white handkerchief. "That'd be the way of it, ordinarily. I generally have my deputies using their horses. This is a different, sort of special situation, however."

"Special?" Luther repeated, puzzled.

"Yep. Your prisoner's a woman," the lawman said.

✻ 3 ✻

Luther stared and swallowed noisily. "A woman?"

"That's what I said," Hollingshead replied. "We get one every once in a while. This one's named Nellie Dupray. Ever hear of her?"

Luther shook his head. "Sure ain't."

"That surprises me some," the sheriff said. "I didn't think there was a man west of the Missouri that hadn't heard of Nellie. Come on, I'll introduce you to her."

Hollingshead moved out from behind his desk and led the way across his office to the door through which Slocum had passed—one that opened into a narrow hallway along one side of which was a row of small cells. The lawman halted at the first in the line, ignoring Chief Deputy Slocum who was standing at the far end of the hall conversing with one of the prisoners.

"Evening, Nellie," Hollingshead said. "Got somebody here you ought to meet."

Daylight had faded and none of the lamps in the corridor had been lit leaving the area deep in shadows. Luther leaned forward, peered through the bars, watched a figure stir and move toward the front of the iron cubicle.

"There's nobody I want to meet unless it's a man bringing me a pardon from the governor."

Nellie Dupray's voice was low, with a dry contemptuous quality as if she found all things beneath her notice and consideration.

Luther shifted nervously as she stepped into full view. Probably in her early thirties, she was a well-built woman with high breasts, a small waist and rounded hips. A wealth of dark hair capped her head and her light-colored eyes were wide set in an oval face. How could a woman so beautiful get herself into such bad trouble, he wondered?

"This is Deputy Luther Pike," he heard the sheriff say. "He'll be the one taking you to the pen."

"Trying to, you mean," Nellie said dryly, sizing Luther up through the bars. "You say he's a deputy? Looks more like he's been working as a scarecrow in some sodbuster's cornfield."

Luther felt his cheeks heat up. Nellie had a mighty sharp tongue—but he reckoned she was right. He did look like anything but a lawman.

"Never you mind," Hollingshead said. "He'll get you to the warden."

"I doubt it," the woman snapped. She was wearing a high-necked, ankle length dress of some soft tan-colored material, and each time she moved her body underneath it seemed to sort of flow.

"You still figuring your friends'll be waiting for you somewhere along the road?"

Nellie laughed, a rich sound in the quiet jail. "You'd sure like to know that for sure, wouldn't you, Sheriff?"

"Neither here nor there," Hollingshead said, indifferently. "All the same to me. The kind of lawmen that work for me don't lose their prisoners. Pike here'll get you to the pen all right. Make up your mind to that, Nellie."

"Sure, sure," the woman said with a deprecating wave of her hand. "When am I going to get some supper?"

"Pretty soon now, I expect," the lawman said. He nodded to Slocum. The deputy immediately departed by a door at that end of the hall, apparently to make the necessary arrangements for the prisoners' evening meals.

Nellie had not noticed. "Well, tell them to hurry it up—and bring along something for me to drink with it."

A yell of approval went up from the heretofore quiet occupants of the cells farther down the row.

"Goes for me, too, Sheriff!" one shouted.

"I'll take whiskey with my grub!" another voice added.

"Same here!" a third declared.

The lawman, paying no attention to the prisoners, studied Nellie until the racket died down. Then, "You'll get coffee, same as everybody else," he said, and nodding to Luther, he turned away.

Nellie's scathing voice reached after him. "Just what I expected from a two-bit jail like this one! Other places I've been in knew how to treat a lady!"

"You tell him, Nellie!" a prisoner shouted as Hollingshead and Luther passed through the doorway back into the office. "Give him hell!"

The lawman halted beside his desk, his broad face in a dark frown. "Could be something to what Nellie's saying," he murmured. "About some of her friends trying to help her, I mean. She's got more friends than a dog's got fleas. Sure wish I had an experienced man to put on this job—"

"Now don't you worry none, Sheriff!" Luther exclaimed, feeling a surge of alarm. "I'll get her to that warden come fire, flood or tick fever. You can bet on it!"

He could have added that he knew his future as a lawman depended on his making a success of the mission, but he let it pass. Hollingshead would know that without being told.

The lawman shrugged, moved in behind his desk and settled onto his swivel chair. "That's how it'll have to be anyway. Nobody else to handle the job."

Luther relaxed, relieved. "What did this Nellie do?" he asked as Hollingshead began to rummage about in the top drawer of the desk.

"Rustling—"

Luther's jaw sagged. "She's a rustler?"

"Well, in a roundabout way," the lawman explained. "She was put on trial with the three men she's been running with. Names are Potts, Grubbs and Farr. Know any of them?"

Luther shook his head as a strain of worry stirred through him. It seemed that every time the sheriff asked him a question along that line, he had to say no. He hoped the man wouldn't suddenly decide he was too dumb to be a deputy, but truth was he just never was much of a hand to stray very far from his work on the Circle H.

"No matter," the sheriff continued. "They blew in here from Texas, teamed up with Nellie and got in the cattle stealing business. Were caught red-handed in the act—

Farr and his two friends doing the actual rustling, Nellie doing the selling.

"Had quite a system working. Nellie would line up a buyer, telling the fellow she was a widow and had to sell off her stock. Then she'd sweet talk him into giving her a big price for the cattle without asking any questions. Never failed—leastwise it didn't most of the time."

"Farr and the others—they already on their way to the pen?"

Hollingshead, now holding a deputy sheriff's star in his fingers procured from the confusion filling the drawer, stared.

"Hell! Around here we don't send rustlers to the pen— we hang them. You know that!"

"Yeh, but if this Nellie had a hand in it—"

"We don't hang women around here, either. You ought to know that, too, Deputy!"

"Yeh, wasn't thinking, I reckon," Luther said, heavily. Somehow he just couldn't seem to say the right things or come up with the correct answers for Hollingshead. "Something else," he added after a bit. "These friends you figure'll maybe try to take my prisoner away from me —why weren't they caught along with the others?"

"Was only three in the bunch that the posse nailed that day. If there are others they weren't taking a hand in that particular deal—and I'm not so sure there are others. Could be all talk on Nellie's part—but you best not bank on it. She's got one hell of a lot of friends and there's plenty of them that might take it in mind to help her . . . Here's your star."

Luther took the bit of metal gingerly, staring at it as if it were the Holy Grail.

"I'm going to suggest you keep it in your pocket 'til you've delivered Nellie to Warden Slope. It'll attract no attention that way—and maybe spare you a peck of trouble."

"Yes, sir."

"Now raise your right hand and I'll swear you in," Hollingshead said, and when Luther had complied, they went through the necessary ritual.

The formality concluded, Luther smiled broadly. He was a sure-enough, honest-to-heaven lawman now! His career was actually beginning—he was starting up his own glory road, as Windy Jackson had put it. The future he'd dreamed of lay before him.

"You finding a joke in this?"

The sheriff's voice had a slight edge. Luther hastily shook his head. "No, was just sort of feeling pleased with myself. Wearing a star and being a lawman's something I've always wanted . . . This all there is to becoming a deputy?"

"I'll give you some papers—mostly ones you'll hand over to the warden when you get there. And there's an identification you'll have to carry—proof that you are a genuine deputy sheriff. Now and then you'll run across some jasper who'll doubt you."

Luther nodded slowly. He was still looking at his badge, reading and re-reading the black letters imbedded in its shining five-pointed face: DEPUTY SHERIFF. The words seemed to glow, to fill him with a fresh determination.

He'd get Nellie Dupray to Capitol City and the Territorial Penitentiary nearby—no matter how many friends she had waiting along the road to help her! He'd not fail Sheriff Hollingshead or the oath he'd sworn to uphold just as he'd never bring disgrace to his star. He was a lawman —and he'd prove he was a good one.

"Keep a sharp eye on any passengers that get on the coach with you—and on the road as well," the sheriff was saying. "You can look for help from the shotgun rider, if you need it. Name's Hazen Webb. I've already told him you'd be aboard with Nellie. Told the driver, too. His name's Jasper Jones—but you can't expect much from him if something starts; he'll be busy handling his team."

"How long a ride is it to the pen?"

"Couple of days. You'll head east out of here, make connections at Connorsville with the north-bound coach. That'll be the only time you'll change. Best you not show yourself or Nellie any more than necessary when you make the transfer—or any other time, far as that's concerned."

Luther frowned. "Don't hardly see how we can swap stagecoaches without—"

"You'll figure out a way. It'll come to you," the sheriff said, confidently. "Now, you'll be needing some expense money. Here's twenty-five dollars. I figure that'll be enough to see you there and back."

"Ought to be a plenty!" Luther agreed, flushing with pleasure. Expense money! He hadn't expected any—and here he was dropping two gold eagles and five silver dollars into his pants pocket.

Hollingshead got to his feet. "Now, I don't want to

upset and worry you, Deputy Pike, but I feel I best say it
again—keep your eyes open every inch of the way to Capitol City, and the pen, once you leave here in the
morning."

"I aim to—"

"Nellie Dupray's tricky as a she fox with a den full of
little ones. You give her just half a chance and it'll end up
with her taking you somewheres, instead of you taking
her.

"I want you to always remember this—the worst thing
that can happen to a lawman is for him to lose his prisoner. It doesn't make any difference how it happened or
how high the odds against him were—it's something he'll
never live down. Once it's done, he'd just as well turn in
his star and forget about being a lawman. His reputation's
ruined forever."

"You can depend on me," Luther murmured.

"Figured I could," the sheriff said crisply, "otherwise
I'd never sworn you in. Now, I want you to go over to the
Drover Hotel, rent yourself a room for the night. Can get
your supper there, too. Tell Ed Hixson—he runs the place
—that I sent you and that you're working for me. Get
yourself a good night's sleep and be here in my office an
hour before daylight in the morning, ready to board the
stage with your prisoner. Clear?"

"Yes, sir," Luther said, feeling full and rich as he
turned for the door. "You can depend on me—I'll be
here."

※ 4 ※

They were the lone passengers climbing into the east-
bound stagecoach that next morning. In the crisp, clear
air Nellie shivered slightly as she paused at the step and
looked back at Tom Hollingshead.

"Don't be looking for me to say you've been nice to me,
Sheriff. Never did enjoy being locked up, no matter how
good the jail was. But I'll say this—you treated me decent."

"Way I do all my prisoners—"

"Maybe, but you can't say that about all lawmen, specially when it comes to a woman. Sometimes it's like
being around a bunch of rutty dogs. But you were decent
—I'll say it again—and I'm glad you won't be getting
blamed when it happens."

Hollingshead's eyes narrowed. "When what happens?"

Nellie gave him an oblique smile. "Never you mind,
Sheriff. Just be plenty glad you'll be setting in your office
where you won't get hurt."

The lawman swung a worried glance to Luther. "You
sure—" he began and then broke off, shrugging. He was
remembering no doubt that he had no choice for the
chore other than Luther Pike.

"Climb aboard you two if you're riding with me,"

Jasper Jones called down from the box. His voice was impatient, sharp. "I ain't waiting all day!"

Nellie smiled again at Hollingshead, and lifting her skirt calf high, placed a dainty foot on the circular iron step, grasped the window sill in one hand, the door frame in the other and drew herself into the coach. Luther started to follow, hesitated, looked back to Hollingshead.

"You reckon I ought to handcuff her?"

The lawman stirred, rubbed at his jaw. "Up to you, Deputy. She's your prisoner. She's been searched—by my wife, of course—and she's not carrying any concealed weapons. Was it me, I'd not use the irons. Attract less attention to her."

"What I was thinking," Luther said, and shifted his eyes to Jasper Jones. "Anybody tries stopping us, driver, like blocking the road, or something, you run right through them. Hear?"

Jones shifted a cud of tobacco to the opposite cheek, squinted sourly at Luther. "Sonny, I was driving one of these things when you was crawling around wetting three-cornered pants. Expect I know what to do when it needs doing."

"Not saying you don't," Luther replied coolly, "but I'm responsible for an important prisoner, and I don't want nothing wrong happening."

"I know what you're doing—sheriff's done told me all about it," Jones said. "Now, you getting in or you staying?"

"I'm getting in," Luther replied, and nodding to Hollingshead, climbed in beside Nellie and jerked the door closed.

He had barely seated himself when the coach leaped forward, rocking back and forth violently on its leather thorough braces. Jasper Jones' voice came down to him, high and shrill, the sound punctuated by the dry, gunshot-like crack of the whip, the steady drumming of the horses' hooves, the whine and grate of the iron-tired wheels. Dust began to seep through the floor boards, hanging restlessly in the coach. Nellie sniffed, brushing at her face with a handkerchief.

"This is going to be a hell of a ride," she said in a tone of disgust. "I hope the boys don't take too long in coming for me."

Luther's mouth tightened. Drawing his pistol, he held it ready in his lap. "Ma'am, you best forget that. You ain't going nowhere excepting to the penitentiary."

Nellie eyed him in quiet amusement as the stage rocked and swayed over the rough road. "You're nothing but a greenhorn, Deputy," she said, finally. "I feel right sorry for you."

"Don't go wasting your sorries on me," Luther replied stiffly. "I reckon I'll manage."

"Manage to wind up in a hole in the graveyard you mean!" Nellie said, voice thick with sarcasm. "If you wasn't so dumb, you'd know why you're here instead of the sheriff or his other deputy."

Luther gave that consideration. Outside the confines of the coach Jasper Jones' voice continued to be an overriding sound on the warming air as he alternately shouted curses and encouragements to his team.

"Well, I'll tell you," Nellie said, steadying herself with the hanger strap as the coach slammed down into an arroyo, lurched up the opposite side. "They didn't want the job. Knew they'd never get me to the pen."

"Could be," Luther said stubbornly, "but I'll sure get you there."

Nellie laughed. "You got about as much chance doing that as hell has of freezing over!" she scoffed. "If I was you, Deputy—what was your name, anyway?"

Luther's anger was building slowly under the lash of Nellie Dupray's scornful tongue and attitude, but he was determined she'd not get him riled—and he'd give her tit for tat.

"You know what it is," he said. "The sheriff told you."

Nellie rocked back on the seat. The coach had leveled off once more. "Oh yes—Luther something-or-other. Well, Luther something-or-other, you best be looking at the country as it goes by because you're seeing it for the last time. Once my friends show—"

"Lady," Luther cut in bluntly, "you just as well hush up about your friends and quit saying things like that. You ain't scaring me one whit—and I'm getting plumb tired of you gabbling on like an old turkey hen."

Nellie gave him a quick, somewhat surprised look, and turning away, fell to viewing the fleeting landscape in silence from her side of the coach.

Luther felt a bit guilty at being forced to speak to a woman in such harsh terms, but the way he saw it she had it coming. He always believed that folks who did a lot of sharp tonguing and jabbing at others, had best be able to take it when somebody started handing it back to them in like manner.

The stage rolled on through the growing morning, at

times running smooth and free across a flat, other times bouncing and jolting along on a rock-studded road, or reeling violently as it negotiated a dry wash. Audible above it all was the voice of Jasper Jones shouting to his horses, urging them on while the coach cracked and creaked under the strain.

Every few miles Luther would pull himself to the window, remove his hat, and thrusting his head through the opening, have his look at the country ahead for possible trouble. He saw no riders at any time, finally concluded that if Nellie did have friends, and they intended to make a try at rescuing her they were planning to wait until later on—possibly after darkness settled in or maybe not until the transfer to the north-bound stagecoach was made.

Whatever, he'd be ready for them. He'd keep his gun out where it'd be handy, and the sheriff said he could depend on the shotgun rider for help. Too, old Jasper Jones would make it mighty hard for anybody to stop the coach. Drivers took being held up, for any reason, personally, and judging from the exchange of words he'd had with Jasper, Luther reckoned the old man was about as touchy as a range bull with no heifers when it came down to something like that.

"I'm sorry if I've been saying a lot of wrong things to you, Deputy—"

At Nellie's apologetic tone Luther turned to her. He hadn't noticed earlier, but she'd tied a blue scarf around her head to hold her dark hair in place, and the effect was very fetching.

"It's all right, ma'am. Expect I was a mite hateful, too."

"You're only doing what you figure's your bounden duty," she continued in the same kindly manner. "What I was trying to say was that I'm sorry for you because of the trick the sheriff is playing on you. I wasn't putting you down or anything like that. I just felt that it wasn't right that you should be getting such a raw deal."

"Knew what I was getting into," Luther mumbled, defensively. "I wasn't sleeping when the sheriff swore me in."

"I'm sure you weren't—and that makes it all the sadder because it shows how much courage you've got. Now, you can't tell me it didn't take a lot of that knowing all the time that you'd be going up against a stacked deck."

"I'll make it, ma'am," Luther said, doggedly.

His temper was again beginning to rise. Nellie hadn't been able to get to him by jabbing, now she was trying soft-soap and being real sweet and friendly. Well, let her. It wasn't going to get her anywhere.

"If you're aiming to bamboozle me," he said, deciding to let her know she was wasting her breath, "you can just forget it. I got a serious job to do, and I aim to get it done come no matter what."

Nellie nodded, pausing to recover herself as the coach rocked wildly to one side, seemingly almost overturning, righted itself and rushed on.

"I can tell you're that kind of a man, all right," she said, brushing at her lips with the handkerchief, "and I certainly do admire you for it. About all else I can say is, well, good luck when the time comes."

"Time comes for what?" Luther asked. He figured he

knew what she meant but he wanted her to spell it out plain for him.

"For when my friends show up to take me away from you. That'll mean plenty of trouble—you can bank on it, because they're not letting me go to the pen, Deputy Luther Pike!"

He grinned, not at the implied threat but at the *Deputy Luther Pike*. It sure had a fine ring to it, and he was wishing Percy Gilmore could have been around to hear Nellie Dupray say it. If he had then maybe Percy would understand why he had changed his way of life and become a lawman.

"You best not do much planning along that line," he said, pulling himself from such pleasant contemplation and facing up to duty. "It ain't going to happen. You're my prisoner, and you're staying that way 'til we get to the pen."

Nellie smiled, once more brushed the dust film from her lips. "You go right on believing that, Deputy, but when the bullets start flying and a couple of them knock you over and you start bleeding like a hog with its throat cut, just you remember that I warned you."

Luther swallowed, managed a smile. "Yes'm, I'll sure do that," he said, endeavoring to sound unimpressed. "Howsomever, you best not—"

The pound of Hazen Webb's shotgun butt on the front of the coach broke into Luther's words. Something was wrong. Suddenly taut, pistol ready in his hand, he drew himself up to the window and glanced out.

"What's the trouble?" he shouted above the thunder of the horses.

"Ain't none!" Webb yelled back. "Just wanting you to know we're stopping. Way station up ahead."

"Obliged," Luther replied and started to settle back when the shotgun rider's voice continued.

"Appears we got a passenger waiting."

✳ 5 ✳

Luther paused. Jaw tightening and eyes narrowing, he again thrust his head out of the window and looked beyond the horses and the swirling dust being churned up by them. The way station, a small hut with a portico, a corral and a lean-to shelter for the teams, stood a few yards off the road. A man was standing in the shade of the portico, a carpetbag in his hand.

"Just could be one of my friends, Deputy," Nellie said in a silky tone. "It's about the time they'd be showing up."

Luther made no reply, but tension was building within him, quickening his pulse, keying his nerves to a razor edge. He remained as he was, head and one shoulder through the open window, pistol ready, as Jasper Jones, maintaining the continuous but affectionate tirade directed at the horses, swept into the station and drew to a halt.

"You stay right where you are," Luther said, throwing a hard glance at Nellie. Pulling back, he opened the door and warily stepped out. The waiting passenger was now moving up to enter. Beyond him the team change was hurriedly under way.

"Who're you?" Luther demanded bluntly, planting himself squarely in front of the would-be traveler.

The man—medium build, narrow-faced, with small, close set eyes, a drooping mustache and pointed beard—came to an abrupt stop. Dressed neatly in a gray cord suit, white shirt with black string tie, he looked to be anything but an outlaw—but Luther knew he couldn't go by that, and he was taking no chance.

"Name's Page—John Page," the man replied, frowning. He was looking not so much at Luther but at the pistol being held by the deputy. "What's this all about?"

"Where you heading?"

From up on the box the shotgun rider, Hazen Webb, watched quietly. Jones was off seeing to the hitching of the fresh horses, making certain that all was in order and to his liking. Two men were leading the relieved team off toward the corral, and a man who had come from the interior of the way station, was standing in the low doorway. From somewhere nearby a gopher barked shrilly.

"Can't see as it's any of your business," Page said angrily, "but I'm going to San Antone."

"You prove that?" Luther said, and immediately realized it was a fool question.

"Sure, got my ticket right here," Page said, and waved it vigorously. "You going to tell me what this's all about or not?"

"Can you prove your name's Page?" Luther continued, amending his previous question. That was what he'd intended to ask in the first place.

Page gestured toward the way station. "They know me—Hubbard and Ike and Celestino Baca."

Luther shifted his attention to the man who had been watching idly from the doorway but was now advancing across the hardpack. A large, wide-shouldered individual, he wore a deep, puzzled frown on his sun-darkened features.

"I'm Hubbard, the agent here," he said. "What's going on?"

"That's what I'm trying to find out," Page mumbled.

Hubbard leveled his hard eyes on Luther. Small and black, they looked like burned holes in his weathered visage. "Who in hell are you and what do you want?"

"I'm a deputy sheriff, from Linksburg," Luther replied, digging into a pocket for his star and exhibiting it. "I'm taking an important prisoner to the pen—and I'm expecting trouble."

Hubbard shrugged. "Well, you ain't likely to get it from John Page. He owns a ranch west of here. Regular customer."

Luther gave that consideration. *Nellie's got more friends than a dog's got fleas,* Tom Hollingshead had warned. Maybe this Page was just a rancher, but that sure didn't rule out the possibility of his being one of those who intended to help Nellie escape.

"You know Nellie Dupray?" he asked, getting to the heart of the situation.

Page brushed at the sweat rapidly accumulating on his face. Jasper Jones, apparently satisfied with the harnessing, was dropping back to take his place on the box.

"Well, matter of fact, I do," he said hesitantly. "What's that got to do with it?"

The station agent's jaw had dropped. "Say, you don't

mean you've got—" he began and stepping hastily up to the stage, looked in. "By heaven, you have! It's Nellie Dupray sure enough! She's this here important prisoner you're talking about."

Up on the seat of the stagecoach Jones had gathered the lines, laced them properly between his stubby fingers, and with a foot on the brake pedal, was glancing down irritably.

"All right, get aboard, mister, if you're going with me!" he barked.

Page bobbed, moved to the open door. Hubbard, speaking in a low voice to Nellie, pulled back, making room for the rancher to enter. Scowling, suspicious, not at all satisfied with the way things had gone, Luther followed, resuming his seat beside Nellie while motioning for Page to take the one opposite, facing them.

"Ain't sure about you yet," he informed the rancher bluntly. "Aim to keep an eye on you."

The coach tilted back suddenly as the horses lunged into the harness, rocked forward and leveled off as they swung onto the road again. Jasper Jones renewed his high sing-song, and once more dust began to drift about in layers within the coach, and the drum of hooves and grating of wheels filled the air which was steadily growing hotter.

"Good to see you again, John," Nellie said, one hand gripping the window sill, the other resting on her knee. "You're looking fine."

Luther, pistol held firmly in his lap, thumb hooked over the hammer, stared at the rancher fixedly. Page stirred uncomfortably.

"Howdy, Nellie," he said cautiously.

The coach began to sway as its speed increased. Page again brushed sweat from his strained features. Luther flung a quick glance through the window. They were dropping off a mesa, descending into a broad swale, one heavily brushed and marked with bluffs and buttes. If there was to be an attempt made by Nellie's friends to free her, this certainly would be an ideal place, he reasoned. Worry now tagging at his mind, he settled his attention again on the rancher.

"Said you was going to San Antone—I never got a close look at your ticket."

Page muttered something, reached carefully into the inside pocket of his coat and produced the slip of thin cardboard which stated he had paid his fare and handed it to Luther. The deputy gave it a quick, verifying glance and returned it. At his side Nellie Dupray was laughing quietly, the sound barely audible above the creaking of the stage and other noises relative to their passage.

The rancher thrust his ticket back into a pocket, once again mopped at his sweaty face. After a moment he gestured at the weapon Luther was holding.

"You mind putting that thing away?" he said in a wild sort of voice. "Road across here's rough. It might go off."

"It ain't going off unless I pull the trigger," Luther said, bracing himself by spreading his legs and pushing hard against the floor with his feet. "Just you don't give me no reason to do that."

"Me? Why would I—"

"The deputy's a mite nervous, John," Nellie explained.

"First time on a job . . . You know, I was just thinking about that week in El Paso. You remember it?"

Page ran a finger under his collar, nodded. "Yeh, guess I do." He was staring at the muzzle of Luther's pistol which somehow had shifted—probably due to the motion of the stage—and was now pointing directly at him.

"Was at Ruby Tallman's house. You blew in with some cattle buyer and practically took over the place—just the pair of you."

"Yeh, I remember," Page said uncertainly.

"We sure had us a time! I recollect you asking me if I was French—my name being Dupray. Never got to give you an answer because those three cowboys showed up about then and pretty quick the fight started between them and you and your friend."

Page nodded helplessly, tried to sink deeper into his seat under Luther's relentless glare, while Nellie, word by word, made it more evident that the rancher was a good friend of long standing.

"Never did answer your question. Well, truth is I ain't French a'tall. Name's really Nellie Calkins. My pa was one of those hell's fire and damnation Baptist preachers, and every time he gave me a hiding for something he didn't approve of, he'd finish up saying, 'Now, Nellie, do pray for your sinful soul and ask forgiveness for what you done.'

"I can't remember ever doing that, but after I ran off and was wanting a new name I thought of the *do pray* part, and because it sort of sounded French, I used it and started calling myself Nellie Dupray."

John Page once more relieved the sweat trapped under

his collar with a circling forefinger, finishing by wiping his mouth with the back of a hand.

"I see," he murmured, but it was obvious he'd paid little mind to what the woman had said, his attention still claimed by the big forty-four lying ready in Luther's lap.

Unexpectedly the coach lurched drunkenly to the left side as the right hand wheels struck a large rock. Dust exploded from its floor and the wood crackled and popped as if coming apart at the joints. The big vehicle slewed back and forth, bouncing, rocking, threatening each moment to overturn, but finally it settled back, and straightening out, raced on to the accompaniment of Jasper Jones' yelling, the steady hammer of hooves and the whine of spinning wheels.

It was enough for John Page. He drew himself to the window of his seat, thrust his head through and shouted to Jones.

"Driver—let me off at your next stop," he directed, and settled back.

Luther eyed him narrowly. "Thought you was going to San Antone—"

Page nodded exhaustedly. "I am—but I'm taking the next stagecoach. Being in this'n—with you setting there holding that pistol on me—is just too much for my nerves!"

❈ 6 ❈

John Page was a man who stuck to his vow. Shortly after midday, when the stage halted at Simm's Crest, this time to only pick up box lunches for the passengers and crew, the rancher bolted hurriedly from the coach and was seen no more. It was a relief to Luther. The fact that Page had not questioned Nellie as to why she was being taken to the pen would seem to indicate that he knew all about it, and that in itself made him suspect.

The stage was underway again in only minutes, Simm's Crest being no regular stop on the schedule except to take on the already prepared food—two meat sandwiches and a tin cup of coffee which was cold by the time they had covered the first hundred yards—if the lurching and pitching of the coach as it made its way back onto the road had left any remaining in the cup.

"Reckon we lost your friend," Luther said in a pleased sort of voice as he bit into his sandwich. The sliced beef was stringy, needed considerable chewing.

"Maybe," Nellie replied coyly. "How do you know but what he got on just to size things up, see who and how many deputies were looking after me? Dropped off then at Simms to join up with the rest of the boys, let them know how things stand."

"He was going to San Antone," Luther countered. "I seen the ticket."

"Maybe that was a trick to fool you, throw you off your guard."

Luther grinned, shrugged. "Nope, he was a mighty scared rabbit. We've seen the last of him."

Nellie paused, suddenly began to laugh. "He sure was, wasn't he? Stood out in his eyes like a flag being waved by a railroader. It was all I could do to keep a straight face!"

Nellie continued to laugh as she thought back over the preceding hours during which the rancher had occupied the seat opposite. But Luther, also reviewing those same minutes was recalling the tension and worry and now was seeing little humor in it.

"I don't appreciate your ragging me," he said roughly as the coach, hurrying on, began to descend into a broad, wild sink.

Nellie sobered. Her shoulders stirred under the smooth fabric of her dress. "Why don't we just say that I'm preparing you for what's to come later."

"Now or later, it'll be all the same to me," Luther said with a show of indifference, cramming the second sandwich into the pocket of his jacket. The first was far from tasty, and the second would be no better, but it might come in handy later.

Nellie smiled again, lay back against the seat, all the while bracing herself by holding onto the window sill.

"I watched John looking at your pistol. I imagine the muzzle looked as big as a silver dollar to him—and every time the stage would jolt and you'd flop around a bit, he'd go white as a sheet!"

Luther permitted himself a half smile, but he was not lowering his guard. For all he knew Nellie Dupray was trying to work something on him—a different kind of charm, being real friendly and gay and the like; Sheriff Hollingshead warned him that she was plenty tricky. Well, the sheriff needn't worry—he wasn't being taken in. But he supposed he might as well go along with the conversation, be congenial. They'd be riding together for a lot of miles.

"I can see now that Page was nothing more than a customer of yours," he said. "Real sorry I had to act the way I did, but there wasn't nothing else I could do. Far as I knew he come aboard and was looking for a chance to throw down on me so's you could get away—and that's something I ain't about to let happen!"

"You going to treat every passenger that climbs aboard like that?" Nellie asked, tossing the remains of her sandwich, as well as the supplementary one, out the window and sipping at the coffee in her near-empty cup.

"Reckon so, unless I know for sure they ain't lined up with you."

Nellie sniffed, brushed at the dust on her face with her handkerchief.

"You better figure on being real busy then, Deputy. I've probably gone to bed with more men than you've ever seen, so we'll be running into friends of mine behind every post."

"I can handle them," Luther said quietly. He glanced through the window. The afternoon was still young, but he thought he might as well get his plan set for when they met the north-bound stagecoach and made the transfer.

"We'll be pulling into Connorsville about supper time," he said, coming back around to face Nellie. "Be changing stages there."

Nellie merely raised her thick brows, let them fall. The dust was worse down in the sink and the heat had increased considerably. She now held the handkerchief to her lips continually.

"So?"

"When we get to the edge of town, you and me are getting off—"

"We what?" Nellie exclaimed, rocking forward.

"I'm having the driver stop and let us out," Luther explained patiently. "Like as not there'll be some of your friends hanging around the station, waiting and watching for us to come in. I don't aim to accommodate them, let them see you. That way they won't be trying anything."

"But if we get off, how're we going to keep on going north?"

"Aim to get back on the northbound at the other end of the town. Can't be much of a walk—and I'll tell Jones to have the other driver looking for us."

Nellie sighed deeply, settled back. "You're crazy, Deputy," she said wearily, dabbing at her cheeks.

"No, guess not," Luther said. "Just using my common sense like the sheriff said I ought, and doing my job."

"Well, I can save you all the trouble you're going to and spare us a lot of useless walking in this heat," Nellie said, perking up. "There won't be any of my boys at Connorsville. They'll be waiting up the line a ways. I'm not saying where, but—"

"Obliged, but we'd best do it my way," Luther said indifferently. "Anyways, walking'll do us some good, sort of rest us up for the ride on to Capitol City and the pen. All this setting around sure cramps a fellow's muscles."

"But there's no need!" Nellie protested, not letting it drop. "There won't be any trouble, Deputy—I promise you!"

"No thank you, ma'am," Luther said coldly. "I ain't listening to none of your promises! I'm doing what I know's safe and right, so you just as well settle down and get it in your mind that we'll be doing it like I say."

Nellie sighed again, leaned back. "Guess it's to be a little like getting raped," she muttered. "Might as well relax and enjoy it."

Luther stared at her. "How's that, ma'am?"

The woman stirred, looked off through her window. She was apparently in no mood to repeat her barroom observation.

He continued to study her for a few moments and then turned from her to put his attention on the rushing landscape outside the coach. The rocks, clumps of rabbit brush, Apache plume, bitter brush, snakeweed, blossoming cholla cactus, were little more than a blur as the stage raced on for its destination, still hours away, to the east.

Jasper Jones, as if tired, no longer shouted at his six-up, and Webb, evidently a quiet man, had given no indication of his presence since warning them of their approach to the way station.

All was going as expected, Luther reckoned, insofar as

he and his prisoner were concerned. She had not given him any trouble, particularly, although he reckoned she'd tried hard enough to yammer him around to her way of thinking, but her words had all slid off his back like rain on a duck.

And there'd been no outside trouble on her behalf, at least so far. He hadn't really expected it until they were aboard the north-bound coach, however, not because Nellie had hinted that was where her friends would be waiting, but mainly because that would be the logical area.

But it was only smart to be on his toes all the time—every foot of the way—and not put too much faith in logic. A man could get fooled every once in a while depending on logic, and he had long since made up his mind that it wasn't going to happen to him.

He wasn't letting anything queer his chances of becoming a good deputy and forging ahead to a fine career as a sheriff—and then U. S. Marshal. That was his ultimate goal—United States Marshal—and he'd make it, only he hadn't realized that being a lawman could be so wearing on a man's nerves. It seemed to him that—

Luther's thoughts broke off abruptly. Through the gray dust haze swirling about the coach, he thought he saw a rider bearing down upon them from a slope to their right. And then, faintly, he heard popping sounds. It dawned on him immediately that they were being fired upon. That became more evident at once when he heard several dull thuds on the side of the coach.

"We're being jumped!" he yelled, turning angrily to Nellie. "Them friends of yours are shooting at us. They ain't caring who they hit—even you!"

And then as the stage suddenly began to pick up speed, the unfamiliar voice of the shotgun rider Hazen Webb reached them.

"Indians! You folks get down on the floor—and stay there!"

7

At once the crackle of Webb's rifle began to fill the coach. Luther drew back from the window and crouched on the floor. He twisted about. Nellie Dupray was still upright on the seat. A frown clouded her face as if she could not understand what was taking place.

"Get down here!" he shouted, and seizing her by the wrist, he drew her to the floor beside him.

The coach was now swaying dangerously as Jones called upon his team for greater speed. The yelling of the Indians had become audible above the protesting creaks and groans of the vehicle, and the sound of gunfire was like firecrackers being set off on Independence Day, rapid and distant.

"Indians—I thought they were all peaceful, that we weren't ever again going to have trouble with them," Nellie said, bracing herself as best she could. It was as if she had finally realized the precariousness of their situation.

"They are—mostly," Luther said, pulling off his hat and moving over to where he could see out one of the door windows. "This is probably a bunch of renegades that've busted off from a main tribe. They've got their outlaws same as we have."

"Apaches, you think?" There was a note of special fear in the woman's voice.

He nodded. "Chiricahuas, I expect," he said tensely. The stage was rocking so badly that he was having trouble staying partly upright. "Could be Mescaleros—or even a bunch of Comanches. Stay down low."

Holding to the sill of the window, Luther looked out. They were racing along a fairly straight road that skirted a deep arroyo. Dust was a yellow-gray curtain surrounding them but he was able to make out three Indians, near naked copper bodies glistening in the sun, racing along behind them. The flat, hollow crack of gunshots coming from off to their left indicated more Indians on that side of the stagecoach.

Abruptly the vehicle veered sharply, slamming Luther against the door, and Nellie Dupray into him. As they recoiled, struggling to regain their cramped positions on the floor between the seat, the stage skidded back into forward motion and again began to whip from side to side.

The sound of Hazen Webb's rifle was reaching them no more. Luther frowned. The Indians were moving in closer. Webb should be increasing his fire—unless—

"Something's wrong up there," he said, hanging tight to the door with his right hand and the forward edge of the seat opposite with his left as he sought to keep from losing balance. Nellie was tight against him, arm about his waist, a light film of sweat on her face. "Best I take a look—"

"Deputy!"

The solitary word was a desperate plea above the noise of the fleeing horses and the whining of the wheels.

"That's Webb," Luther said tautly. "Driver must've got hisself shot. Team's running away and Webb's trying to handle them. Means nobody's shooting back at them redskins."

He felt Nellie's encircling arm slacken, and drawing up again to the door, threw a glance to their rear. The Indians—seven of them—were now all behind the coach, seemingly content to follow along in the wake of the wildly yawing vehicle, doing no more than maintaining their distance. Either they were biding their time for a better moment to close in, or they were aware of something ahead that would halt the stagecoach for them; or more Indians could be waiting.

"Dammit all," Luther muttered. Opening the door, he began to work his way forward along the rocking body of the coach toward the box.

It wasn't too hard, and Luther's anger at the Indians for creating a problem in his drive to become a lawman was such that he gave his own recklessness little thought as he clung to the bar of the luggage rack and fought to keep a toe-hold on the edge of the window.

When he had finally managed to get a grip on the hand rail of the driver's seat, and had drawn himself onto it, he saw that he was right. Jasper Jones, a hole in the back of his head, had slipped off the box and lay crumpled on the floor beneath it. One leg hung over the side, swinging grotesquely with the erratic motion of the coach; an arm was draped over the dashboard as if to stabilize the limp body and prevent it from slipping further and falling beneath the wheels.

Webb, crouched low, was holding the lines, doing his best to slow the fear-stricken horses. He was having no success. Turning a grim face to Luther, he smiled.

"Hell of a note!" he shouted. "A bunch of damned redskins—"

"Where's your rifle?" Luther shouted back, bracing himself and looking about.

"Gone. Lost it over the side when Jasper got hit and we nigh turned over. Use your pistol. That's all we got."

Luther glanced back at the Indians. They were no nearer. "Too far—way out of range," he said. "Why you figure they're holding off?"

Webb, sweat streaming from his face, sawed at the reins and jabbed methodically at the brake pedal with his booted foot as he struggled to slow the careening stage. He shook his head.

"Don't know. Could maybe have themselves some friends waiting down the road a piece."

Luther nodded. "Kinda got that idea myself," he said, and reaching over drew Hazen Webb's pistol from its holster.

"Ain't no sense wasting lead on that bunch trailing us," he said, brushing at his eyes to wipe away the dust and moisture, "but maybe we can bust right through any that's blocking the road."

"Maybe," Webb said. "Ain't sure I can hold the team much longer. Arms are coming off, seems like, but if I let up a bit, give them their heads any more'n they've already took, they'll wreck us sure."

"Want me to spell you?" Luther offered. Legs spread, both feet jammed against the dash, he was rocking from side to side as the coach plunged on down the slight grade at top speed.

"Can't chance handing you the lines yet," the shotgun rider replied. "First climb we reach they'll start slowing and the drag'll be against them. Be obliged if you'll take over then . . . Your prisoner—she all right?"

"Was when I left her," Luther answered. To talk was difficult, it being necessary to shout in order to be heard, and the dust whipping up from the horses' hooves and dripping off the tires of the spinning wheels was filling their throats with a powdery dryness.

Again Luther glanced over his shoulder. The Indians were perhaps a few yards closer, but very little. Most likely Hazen Webb was right; there would be more waiting on ahead with plans to block the road and halt the coach. The braves coming along behind were simply there to drive them into what amounted to a trap and prevent any possibility of the coach turning around and trying to retreat to the way station.

"Not—going to be—able to hold—them much longer!" Webb shouted in an exhausted, faltering voice. Sweat now lay in a shining coat on his dark, weathered features and his eyes, tortured by dust and sun, were squeezed down to mere slits.

"I'll spell you anytime!" Luther offered again.

The stage was whipping badly. The creaking and crackling of the wheels gave warning that the spokes could give way at any instant as the weight of the vehicle was thrown alternately against them from the side. But they were helpless to do anything about it; there was no slowing the madly running horses.

In the harsh, driving sunlight their bodies glistened with sweat and flecks of froth from their gaping jaws continually drifted back, while their legs were no more than blurs. A thought came to Luther as he fought to stay on the seat.

"We come to that roadblock, we ain't going to slow that team," he said. "Way they're running nothing short of a wreck'll do it."

"Expect you're right," Webb conceded, "but there ain't nothing I can do about it. Just have to take our chances . . . You best climb down, see about your prisoner."

Luther nodded. He wished there was something he could do to assist Webb, but it wasn't possible for the man to pass him the lines with the team running wild as it was; the slightest slack in the reins and they'd turn the coach over for certain. But he felt he should be up there with the shotgun rider turned driver so that he could make use of their two pistols in the event they had to run a gauntlet of waiting Indians.

"I'll warn her—tell her to hang on tight," he said, "but I aim to stay here on the box with you so's I can do the shooting when—"

"Look out!" Webb yelled in a high, despairing voice. "We're going over! Jump!"

8

They were at a sharp bend in the road. The arroyo that lay below was deep and studded with rocks and brush. Luther, knowing only that he had to get clear of the heavy vehicle, launched himself from the seat with all his strength, giving no thought to what he might be hurling himself onto.

He heard Nellie scream as the coach sailed off into space, wheels spinning, horses frantically pawing the hot, dusty air as they struggled against their harness; and felt a flash of anger once again for the renegade Indians because of what they were doing to him and his prisoner, and thus to his hopes for the future—and then a hundred sharp points dug into him as he went full length into a squat clump of brittlebush.

The jolt, despite the cushioning effect of the tough, springy shrub, stunned him, but only briefly. Gathering himself, he gained his footing, and holstering the pistol still clutched tightly in his hand—somehow he'd lost Webb's—he glanced about. The coach, splintered, crushed, wheels turning furiously, still attached to the team, lay in a dense cloud of dust a dozen strides away. Taut, he started toward it.

Two of the horses lay quiet, their necks apparently broken; three were on their feet, trembling, looking about dazed but not seriously hurt. The sixth animal was on its side and attempting to rise but one foreleg lay at an odd angle and it was having no success.

Luther, hurrying, gave the team only quick notice as he passed. He saw the crumpled shape of Jasper Jones on beyond the wrecked coach, and then as he drew nearer, caught sight of Hazen Webb's lifeless body, trapped beneath it. Throat tightening, he reached the shattered vehicle, looked inside. There was no sign of Nellie. The woman had apparently been thrown clear or, like him, had managed to jump.

Luther pivoted, urgency and anxiety pressing him hard. The Indians could be only a few yards away, and while their position on the road above would prevent their seeing the destroyed coach until almost upon it, he could expect them to arrive on the scene in only moments.

A groan caught his ear, bringing him about instantly. It was Nellie. She lay half hidden in a stand of feathery-blossomed Apache plume. He reached her in two long bounds, and not taking even a fraction of a moment to examine her, took her in his arms and started down the arroyo at an awkward, staggering run.

The pound of running horses, the shouts of the renegades on the road warned him of their nearness. At once he turned aside from the sandy center of the big wash and ducked in behind a stand of thick rabbit brush.

Sucking hard for wind, Luther laid the woman out flat, threw his glance toward the coach and the rim of the arroyo above it. The Indians were moving slowly along, glancing down, as they rode toward a place where they could descend. He didn't think they had seen him—and hoped he was right. He'd have no chance against so large a party in a head-on shoot-out—and that's what it would amount to.

Nellie stirred. Luther shifted his attention to her. She opened her eyes, stared up at him wonderingly, started to voice a question. He shook his head warningly, pointed toward the coach. "Indians," he whispered. "You hurt any?"

Nellie's face was scratched and her hair had come down and was in thick folds about her neck and shoulders. She shook her head. "The others?"

"Driver got hit by a bullet. Webb, the shotgun rider's dead, too. Caught under the stage when it hit."

A wry, cynical smile parted Nellie's lips. "Just my luck. They're both dead, and you're still alive. Why couldn't it've been the other way around?"

Luther passed the remark off with a shrug. "We could both be dead—or laying out there waiting for them renegades to carve us up."

Nellie, now sitting up, looked away. She apparently hadn't considered that possibility. Turning, she faced him.

"How'd I get here? Did you carry me?"

Luther nodded, his eyes on the Indians. They had made the descent from the road somewhere on beyond the sharp curve, had ridden up to the coach and were now dropping from the backs of their ponies to begin poking about in the wreckage.

One halted by the wounded horse, renewing its frantic

efforts to regain its feet. The brave drew a knife from his waistband, slashed the animal's throat, and moved on toward the three unhurt horses standing quietly in the harness. Again using his knife the Indian cut them free of the trailing straps that pinned them to the dead ones, and using a length of the reins, tied them to a clump of brush. That bit of salvage completed, the brave doubled back to rejoin his friends.

The renegades appeared to be disappointed with their prize. They had found little of value to them other than the horses, and since there was no baggage they were forced to the conclusion that the stage was carrying no passengers.

"I'm obliged to you for getting me away from there," Nellie murmured, watching the braves as they probed the area indifferently for something overlooked earlier. "I'd hate to end up in the hands of savages like them. What they do to a white woman, they say, is—"

"I wasn't about to lose my prisoner," Luther cut in, now having his small moment of revenge for her remark concerning her ill luck at his being alive. "Still figure to deliver you to that warden at the pen."

Nellie brushed hair away from her face, shining from a thin film of sweat. "With them out there? You're loco, Deputy. We're not going anywhere."

"Not right now, maybe. Later I expect we will."

The woman shrugged, began to work at her hair, pulling and tucking it into place while shaping her scarf to do double duty as a bonnet to protect her face from the sun and still hold her dark tresses in place. Luther kept his attention on the Indians. There was a chance one would notice the tracks he'd left in the sand as he hurried off with the unconscious Nellie in his arms. Fortunately the renegades would not be looking for others, he reasoned; the absence of baggage, which would have indicated passengers aboard, was a big factor in their favor.

The Indians had taken the bodies of Jones and Hazen Webb, stripped them, and after claiming what personal effects they fancied, turned to their ponies. Mounting, they rose lazily off into the direction from which they had come, their guttural voices as they conversed carrying plainly to Luther and Nellie. The brave who had seen to the captive horses at the outset, hurriedly freed them, and using the lines as lead ropes, followed.

When all were out of sight, Luther came to his feet. "We've got to pull out of here fast," he said. "Can you walk all right?"

Nellie drew herself upright, took a few tentative steps, nodded. "I guess so. A little sore in places. Which way are we going—toward Connorsville or back to that last way station?"

Luther swiped away the sweat on his face with a forearm. "Neither one. We'll head north. There's bound to be a ranch close by. We can borrow a couple of horses."

"Makes better sense to head for Connorsville," Nellie declared stubbornly. "Can't be too far."

"About three hours by stagecoach running fast, from here," Luther said. "That adds up to a lot of miles. Got to stay clear of the road, anyway. Those redskins are keeping watch over it, and right now, they aren't far from here. Come on."

Not waiting to see if she followed, Luther stepped out

from behind the brush and doubled back over his tracks
to the wreckage. They would have to pass by it, climb the
slope and cross the road if they were to strike north, and
that seemed the smartest thing to do. Connorsville was
too far, as he'd pointed out to Nellie, and the distance to
the last stagecoach stop was even greater—and there was
nothing south. Besides, their destination lay to the north.

Luther paused, glanced at the bodies of Jasper Jones
and Hazen Webb, wishing there was time to give them a
proper burying. But it was out of the question; to delay
longer in the area could prove to be a fatal mistake. The
renegades could return at any moment.

He moved on, halted again, the circular shape of a canteen, the property of Webb or Jones, catching his eye. It
lay half under the coach where it had escaped the attention of the Indians. Hurrying to it, Luther pulled it clear,
and holding it up shook it to assess its contents. It was a
little more than half full, he judged. Again good fortune
had smiled at them; the hike that lay ahead of them
through the dry, burning short hills would be no cinch—
even with ample water.

Hanging the container on a shoulder, he glanced to the
sky. Vultures were already beginning to gather, drawn by
that combination of keen sight and sixth sense with which
they were possessed, and he wished again there was time
to cover the bodies of the two men. He'd make time,
Luther decided suddenly, at least to do that.

Crossing to the coach, he jerked the canvas cover of the
boot free, and carrying it back to where Jones and Webb
lay, placed it over them. Then, picking up several rocks,
he weighted the stiff fabric so that it would not blow off,

and stepped back. At least the bodies were fairly safe from the buzzards and the coyotes—but he knew the canvas would provide no permanent protection.

Again he glanced to the sky, judged the time. Still a couple of hours or so until dark. Night would be most welcome, were it near; they would be much safer insofar as the renegade Indians were concerned—but it was not close and there was nothing he could do about it.

He could get Nellie and himself away from the arroyo with its death and destruction and possibility of further trouble, however, and he reckoned he'd best do it fast. Turning to the woman he beckoned impatiently.

"Let's go—"

She was standing near the coach gazing off in the direction of Connorsville. Her shoulders stirred tiredly under their thin coating of dust.

"You're making a mistake, cutting out across country like you plan to do, Deputy," she said. "We ought to start walking for Connorsville."

"No sense heading that way, risking everything. Not where we aim to go."

She stared at him, frowning. "Capitol City?"

"Yes, ma'am, Capitol City and the pen. We'll get there if we have to walk every step of the way."

Nellie drew herself up rigidly. "Not me, mister! You're not making me walk—not even to the next—"

"Expect you'll do what I tell you," Luther said quietly, taking his handcuffs from a pocket and moving toward her, "else I'll be dragging you along with these irons."

Nellie jerked back from his outstretched hand, swore,

shook her head. "You won't need those!" she said, and then added, "Like I told you before, you're looney!"

Luther returned the cuffs to his hip pocket, smiled ruefully. "Yeh, reckon I am—just looney enough to get you to the pen no matter what! Come on—that there dust to the east could be them Indians."

✳ 9 ✳

Luther moved off with Nellie a few steps behind. After a bit he halted, allowing her to catch up and get ahead. It wasn't that he feared she would attempt to overpower him and escape; hell, what could she do? Nothing! It was simply that he didn't want her lagging and perhaps petering out and dropping far back without him knowing it.

It was hard going. The sand was dry and loose, making their footing difficult; the weeds were stiff and resisting and the sun merciless. After only a hundred yards Nellie stopped abruptly, sat down in the scant shade afforded by a mesquite.

"I'm not going one step farther without some rest," she declared flatly.

Luther shook his head and dropped to his haunches beside her. "It'll take us a week of Thursdays getting somewheres if you're going to be stopping every little bit."

"Little bit!" Nellie echoed, glancing back over the distance they had come. Immediately her manner altered. "I—I guess I'm just not used to walking. I still think it'd be smart to follow the road. Could be some rancher would come along, or maybe even another stagecoach."

"Could be," Luther agreed, "but my guess is that we'd be more apt to run into the Indians again." Raising a hand he gestured toward the east. "That dust's coming closer. I expect that's them."

Nellie frowned, followed his line of sight. "Could just as easy be some rancher—"

"Not with them redskins hanging about—"

"You don't know that for sure!" Nellie said, rising. "Deputy, I'm not moving one more step until I see who that is!"

Luther drew himself upright, considered the distant haze doubtfully. "Be kind of risky staying here. The Indians'll quick see that somebody was there at the wreck after they rode off, and start looking for tracks."

"If it is the Indians—"

Luther sighed, glanced about, settled his eyes on a mound of brush and rock a short distance above them on the adjacent slope.

"Reckon you're going to have your way or else," he said wearily, and pointed to the ragged formation. "Let's get up there where we can hide if it becomes needful. We'll be able to see better, too."

Nellie considered the mound thoughtfully. "I think we ought to double back, get closer to the road. Then if it's somebody that can help us we'll be near enough to attract their attention."

"I can do that easy from right up there," Luther said, patting the pistol on his hip. "Couple of shots in the air will do the trick . . . You for certain you want to do this?"

Nellie looked at him puzzled. "Of course! Why not?"

"I'm still betting that dust's being kicked up by the Indians coming back. And if it is and they spot our tracks and start trailing us we—"

"They won't—mainly because I'm sure it's not them," she said decisively, and started up the slope for the mound. "There just has to be somebody else on that road besides them."

"Not specially. Indians start ambushing pilgrims and stagecoaches and the like, everything stops until it all blows over or the army moves in," Luther said.

He stood for a moment watching her and then fell in behind. There seemed no way to convince the woman that she could be wrong, that the slim possibility she was right was too great a risk to take. He guessed the only answer was to go along with her and hope it was not a mistake. But if it turned out he was right and that she was wrong, he intended to make it clear that from there on they would be doing everything his way and according to his judgment—and with no argument from her.

The climb was short but steep. By the time they reached the brush and moved into it both were breathing hard and sweat was shining on their faces and soaking their bodies. Selecting a rock in the shadow of a rabbit brush, Nellie sat down and began to fan herself with her handkerchief. Luther took up a position back of one of the larger boulders which was further screened by clumps of the gray-green shrub.

"They're getting closer," he said, shading his eyes with a cupped hand as he stared off toward the road. "Leastwise, the dust is."

Nellie made no reply. The brief climb had drained her strength and she was still straining for breath. Luther gave her a moment's study, shook his head. He hoped, strongly, that the dust cloud was being stirred up by someone other than the Indians. Covering any distance on foot across country with Nellie Dupray was going to be next to impossible.

"Can—I have—a drink—please?" she managed after a bit.

Luther stepped back from the rock, and uncorking the canteen, handed it to her. She took a swallow, made a face.

"Warm," she muttered.

He grinned, replaced the stopper. "But it's wet—and that's what counts," he said and returned to his place by the rock.

After several minutes, she moved up beside him. She was breathing normally now and some of the strain had faded from her face.

"Can you tell who it is yet?"

"They're closer," Luther replied, "but I still can't see much. Soon as they come out from behind that shoulder of rock we ought to know who—or what's—kicking up the dust."

"Have you got your gun out and ready to fire a signal?"

"It's ready, don't you fret none about that. I'm hoping we can flag us a ride, or get help, same as you—but I want to get something straight with you. If I'm right and you're wrong, I ain't listening to you no more about what's best to do. We'll do things my way and no back talk. That clear?"

Nellie's shoulders stirred. "If you're right, Deputy," she said, agreeing.

"Good. Just want us to have an understanding. Something else you best know, too; if it's them renegades and

they start looking for us, we're going to have to leave here
plenty fast—and keep going fast. There won't be no stopping every little bit to rest."

Again the woman shrugged. Perspiration was beginning to show through the dress she wore, appearing several places in dark spots. She dabbed at her face, adjusted
the scarf about her head.

"There'll be no need," she said confidently. "You just
be ready to shoot that pistol, make whoever it is stop for
us."

Luther was staring off in the direction of the road. A
half a dozen or so riders had come from behind the bulge
that was blocking his view, moving toward the arroyo
where the stagecoach had wrecked.

"Renegades—it's them!" he said, heavily.

A sigh of disappointment escaped Nellie's lips. She
pressed in close to him, shaded her eyes and looked off
across the heat-laden distance at the riders—small, dark,
coppery figures.

"Are they the same ones, you think?"

"Expect so. They're moving in like they know what's
down there."

One of the renegades had dropped from sight, clearly
having left the road and descending into the deep wash
where the wreckage lay. The others began to follow.

"Was hoping they'd keep going, but they ain't," Luther
said. "Figure to have themselves another look around, I
reckon, and then go on. They'll for sure see somebody's
been there—that canvas I threw over Jones and Webb
will tell them that—and then they'll start hunting for

tracks. Won't take them long to find ours—so we best pull out."

Luther turned away, crossed to a clump of rabbit brush and ripped off a large branch. Nellie, silent, watched him.

"Head down into that, and keep following it," he said, pointing to a narrow wash at the foot of the slope, curving off to the north.

At once Nellie headed down the grade for the arroyo. Luther, throwing a final glance toward the now deserted road, followed, wiping out their tracks with the leafy branch of the rabbit brush as he did.

✻ 10 ✻

It was easier traveling in the wash and they made good time for the first quarter mile. At that point, Nellie, near exhaustion, was forced to halt and rest. Luther, leaving her in the shadow of the arroyo's wall, climbed out and keeping low to avoid being silhouetted against the cloudless, burning sky, made his way to the nearest rise.

A curse exploded from his taut lips. It was as he had feared. The Indians had discovered the signs of their presence at the wreckage, had ferreted out their tracks, and were now in pursuit. In but very little time, Luther realized, they would reach the mound of rocks and brush.

At once he cut back down the slope to where Nellie was resting. "They're coming," he said in a quick, tense way. "We've got to get moving."

Nellie, stretched out full length on the sand, arose at once, alarm tightening her features. "Which way?"

"Keep following the wash," he replied. "Still the best idea—keeps us down low out of sight and the walking's easier. I'll brush out our tracks, like I've been doing, make it hard for them."

They set out immediately, and Nellie in the lead, goaded by fear, maintained a fast, steady walk. Luther, using the bit of rabbit brush continued to wipe out the

traces of their passage—but he knew such would not deter
the Indians for long. Soon they would be where they could
look ahead from higher ground, and by so doing, see the
woman and him. After that it would be only a matter of
time until they caught up, and closed in.

Desperate, sweat soaking him, Luther searched the
country around them anxiously. Shortly they would reach
an area of ragged bluffs and brush-covered, broken hills.
A thread of hope stirred through him. If they could make
it to there before the renegades spotted them, they might
have a chance.

"Up there—the bluffs," he said, drawing up beside the
woman and pointing. "Got to reach there. Be places to
hide."

Nellie only nodded, saving her breath, and hurried on
as best she could. It was hardly necessary to keep brushing out their footprints, Luther felt, but he was looking
for every possible advantage, however thin.

They came to the first of the bluffs, one that overshad-
owed the arroyo they were following. Luther motioned
for Nellie to cut sharp right into the wild, rank growth,
and immediately took extra care to wipe out all indi-
cations of their passage.

They had gone no more than a dozen steps when a yell,
echoing through the hills, reached them. It could mean
but one thing—the renegades had been able to trail them
swiftly despite Luther's efforts to cover their tracks, and
were now almost upon them.

"That ledge—where all that brush is," he said in a low,
urgent voice, and pointing again, indicated a bluff a short
distance in front of them. "We can keep down low, hide

there. If it comes to shooting, it'll be a good place to make a stand, being above the wash."

They gained the ledge, thick with prickly-pear cactus, snakeweed, bitter brush and other wild growth and burrowed their way into it. Sweat-soaked and caked with dust, they waited. From where they lay they could see back up the wash along which they had just come for a short distance, and then follow its course as it passed directly below the ledge to continue on into the low hills.

Abruptly one of the Indians appeared. Astride a wiry gray pony, legs dangling loosely while he studied the ground, Luther recognized him as the brave who had taken charge of the stagecoach horses. He had evidently found evidence of their tracks in the wash, had concluded rightly that the parties they trailed were somewhere along its sandy course.

Another brave appeared, arriving quiet as a shadow. He was riding a fine-looking black that bore an army saddle. Then, in single file the remaining five renegades came into view. Halting in a wide place of the arroyo, they watched silently, leaving it up to the man in the lead to show the way.

When he reached the place where Luther and Nellie had cut away from the wash and climbed to the ledge, he hesitated, after a moment he dropped from his horse, and squatting, examined the sand closely. Then, rising, lean shape bent, head thrown forward, he looked ahead to where the arroyo curved off into the hills. Pivoting suddenly, he vaulted onto the gray. Muttering something to his friends over a shoulder, he moved on, eyes still scouring the floor of the wash.

Motionless, scarcely breathing, Luther watched the Indians pass below him—little more than an arm's length away. Their bodies glistened with sweat, and their coarse, black hair shone dully in the strong sunlight as they trailed after the man on the gray.

The line halted. The last brave was directly below the ledge. Cursing silently, Luther looked to see what had brought about the change. The man in the lead—the tracker—was doubling back. Narrow features set, intent, his hard, dark eyes searched the ground before him relentlessly as he sought to rediscover the telltale footprints they had followed but had somehow lost.

The remaining Indians were quiet for a time, and then as the minutes wore on under the blistering sun, they began to talk back and forth, evidently making none too complimentary remarks concerning the tracker's ability. Finally they became loud, began laughing and pointing while the brave on the black, producing a canvas water bag, took a long swallow and passed the container along.

But it was not water the renegades were drinking, Luther realized, noting their reactions. Probably tizwin, or perhaps white man's whiskey, either stolen or traded for. With each turn at the bag the braves became noisier and more boisterous, but the tracker stubbornly continued to probe, moving about in small circles, kneeling, squatting, touching a bit of sand here and there, all the while paying no mind to the others. Finally he straightened up, shrugged.

A burst of guttural questions was thrown at him. Again his shoulders stirred, and looking off toward the bend in the arroyo, he gestured indefinitely. His meaning was clear; their quarry was somewhere off in the tangle of brush, arroyos and hills ahead.

Luther breathed easier again. The braves would go on now and Nellie and he could, as soon as it was safe, resume their search for a ranch house or homesteader. His relief came to a sudden end. Two of the Indians had dismounted, were standing beside their ponies while they talked and gestured. Evidently they wanted to call a halt, rest a bit in the shade and enjoy more of the water bag's contents before going on.

Luther's jaw set. The Indians were certain to discover him and the woman if they remained there for any length of time, and the brave on the gray who had done the tracking and lost the trail, was sure to renew his probing for sign. Eyes narrowed, Luther studied the party as they wrangled back and forth. He needed to come up with an idea that would induce the renegades to leave; but what?

In the brush, and so near the braves, he dare not attempt the old trick of throwing a rock off into the distant brush to draw their attention. They would hear him, possibly even see him. . . . The brave on the horse directly below the ledge. Luther's thoughts halted there. Slumped on his pony, listening to the argument, he was unmoving as if dozing. His back was to the ledge, as were all the others. The deputy's eyes narrowed as a plan took shape in his mind—a risky one, to be sure, but at least it would give Nellie Dupray and him a chance.

Turning slowly, hugging the ground, Luther looked about until he found a dead branch. Picking it up carefully, soundlessly, he examined it. A taut grin cracked his lips. One end was sharp where it had been broken off from the mother plant. Catching Nellie's attention, he made a jabbing motion with the arm length stick of wood toward the hindquarters of the brave's pony. She frowned, and he wasn't sure if she understood or not.

It didn't matter. They would be found for certain if the party did not move on, and the only answer to that was to force them to do so. Careful, working very slowly, Luther edged to the lip of the ledge. Stick poised, he looked down. The rump of the Indian's horse was immediately below him, well within reach. He glanced at the others. They were still wrangling, apparently unable to decide whether to remain or ride on.

A second thought came to Luther. Drawing his pistol he laid it close by where he could snatch it up instantly if the need arose. It would come down to a shoot-out if his plan backfired, and he wanted to be ready.

He cast a look again at Nellie, grinned faintly when he saw that she was watching him, then, tense, jaw clamped tight, he took a deep breath, raised his arm and drove the pointed end of the stick into the hindquarters of the renegade's horse.

The startled animal leaped upward, came down stiff-kneed with the surprised brave grabbing frantically at the pony's mane as he sought to keep from being thrown. Shouts went up from the other Indians, and the two who had dismounted hurriedly got out of the path of the wildly bucking and plunging horse. Abruptly the frightened animal pivoted, and with its rider's arms clamped about its neck, rushed off down the wash at a fast run. Still laughing and yelling, the other Indians followed.

Luther waited only until the last of the party had disappeared around the bend in the arroyo, and then putting on his hat, lunged to his feet. Wheeling to Nellie, he grasped her hand, pulled her erect.

"We've got no time to waste," he said tautly, starting immediately to move off the ledge. "Redskins'll start wondering what spooked that horse, come back for a look. We sure don't want to be nowheres close by."

White faced, Nellie said, "Go as fast as you want—I'll keep up."

They reached the floor of the arroyo, crossed, climbed the opposite side, Luther again erasing their tracks. Shortly they came to another wash, and dropping into it, followed its winding course until they were out of the bluffs and once again in the short hill country.

And then, a time after that, with the sun beginning to sink behind the ragged horizon in the west, they saw what they were hoping for—a ranch house in the near distance.

11

"Place doesn't look like much, but it's sure a welcome sight," Nellie murmured as they climbed a small rise and had a better view of the ranch house.

"Smoke coming out of the chimney. Somebody living there for sure—and they're home," Luther said, looking back toward the bluffs.

A quick frown pulled at the woman's features when she noted his point of interest. "Those renegades—are you afraid they're following us again?"

He shook his head, removed his hat and ran fingers through his hair, damp from sweat. It was a relief to be walking slow now, to be cool and no longer sweltering under the sun.

"No sign of them," he said. "Expect they headed on back to the road. Better pickings there."

Nellie, attention again on the ranch house, began to work at improving her appearance—straightening her dress, and brushing off the loose dust, rearranging her hair and the scarf that secured it, cleaning her face and neck with a handkerchief wet by water from the canteen.

"That was a real smart trick you pulled to get rid of them," she said, a faint smile toying with her full lips.

"Was a funny sight—that Indian trying to stay on that horse, jumping and bucking like it was."

Luther grinned, remembering the moments; but he had seen no humor in the situation at the time it was taking place. Then there was only breathless tension and an awareness that if the idea, born of desperation, did not succeed, both Nellie and he would be facing torture and death.

"I'm mighty glad it worked," he said, and glanced toward the cluster of buildings huddled in a swale near the foot of a low bluff. "And I'm mighty glad, too, that we come onto this ranch—or homestead. Wasn't craving none to walk all the way to Capitol City and the pen."

Nellie let the comment pass, her gaze on the weathered structures looming up starkly in the closing darkness.

"Now that we're nearer, the place sure don't look like much," she said in a falling voice.

"Can't always go by looks," Luther replied, but he was having misgivings, also.

The main house was small, had a sagging roof and several broken windows that had been repaired by the simple expedient of stuffing rags into the openings. The barn presented an equally dilapidated appearance, but the corral looked strong, the well house sturdy, and standing under a tree near a garden was a fairly good spring wagon. Chickens could be seen wandering about in an enclosed pen off to the side, and the smell of hogs was in the air.

They reached the yard fronting the property, halted at a line of rocks that had been laid to mark off the specific area. Luther stayed the woman with his hand.

"We best not go any closer without being asked," he said, and then called, "Hello, the house!"

There was no response other than the hurried flutter of two disturbed doves that had been resting in a starved-looking cottonwood tree at the corner of the house.

"Hello! Anybody home?" Luther tried again.

"You're dang right we're home!" a harsh voice replied from the depths of the house. "Who are you—and what're you wanting?"

"Name's Pike. I'm a deputy sheriff taking a prisoner to the pen. We got—"

"Where's your horses?" the voice demanded skeptically.

"Wasn't riding none. Were on the stage when a party of Indians—renegade Apaches I suspect—jumped, wrecked the coach. We had to run for—"

"There ain't been no Indian trouble around here in years," the voice cut in flatly. "You're lying."

A squat shape had materialized slowly from the shadows inside the house, becoming apparent in the doorway. It was an old man with a dark, wizened face, small, shoe-button eyes, and a ragged, unkempt beard. He was wearing a dirty undershirt, faded and patched bib overalls, and thick-soled sod-buster shoes. In his gnarled hands he held a double-barreled shotgun with both rabbit-ear hammers pulled to full cocked position.

"Nothing of the kind!" Luther protested angrily. "It's just like I told you. I'm a deputy—"

"You ain't said what you're wanting," the man reminded.

There was more movement in the darkness behind him.

Shortly a woman, probably of the same age, in a worn, colorless dress, stringy, gray hair hanging about her pinched face, eased into view at his shoulder. Luther greeted her with a nod.

"Howdy, ma'am," he said. "Was just starting to tell your mister there we'd like to—"

"We ain't got nothing to give you if you're begging!" the old woman declared in a shrill voice.

Luther shook his head impatiently. What the devil was wrong with folks? Didn't a man being a deputy sheriff mean anything to them?

"If you all'll let me talk, I'll tell you why we're here and what we're wanting," he said in a strong, firm way. "And we ain't begging nothing, ma'am . . . you mind telling me your name? Kind of hard to talk—"

"Oglesby," the man said.

"Fine, Mr. Oglesby. Now, we're getting somewheres. Whether you aim to believe me or not, a bunch of Indians forced the stagecoach we were on to turn over on a bad curve. Killed the driver and the shotgun rider, but we jumped—got throwed clear—and wasn't hurt."

"We barely got away from them," Nellie added. "They chased us for miles—"

"You hearing this, Callie?" Oglesby said, nudging the woman, evidently his wife, with an elbow. "Claim they was set on by Indians."

The woman's thin shoulders stirred. "There ain't been no trouble around here in a long time," she said, virtually repeating his comment. "Expect they're lying about it."

"Just what I told him," Oglesby said, and glaring at Luther, raised the shotgun threateningly. "Get! I'm giving you ten seconds to be off my property! If you ain't—"

"I've got cash money," Luther broke in, patting a side pocket. "Aim to pay."

The old double-barrel lowered tentatively. "Cash? What're you wanting to buy?"

"Like to rent a couple of horses for a few days, buy some grub—"

"Ain't renting no horses—not to you or nobody else," Oglesby stated flatly. "Might sell you my team, the price being right."

Nellie sighed wearily, brushed at her face. Luther frowned, said, "It all right if we come in closer? The lady's tired."

Oglesby motioned with the shotgun's muzzle at the shadows on the east side of the house. "Come on," he said. "Woman can set herself on that bench there if she's of a mind. Just don't try no tricks . . . What about my team?"

"Depends on what you think is the right price," Luther said, and crossing the yard, he halted in the shade. Nellie, walking beside him, immediately found a seat on the crude bench indicated by the homesteader.

"What kind of grub you needing?" Callie asked. "Or was you just talking so's you could get in close?"

"No ma'am, we need it," Luther said. "Like to buy some bread or maybe biscuits, coffee, bacon, spuds, anything else you got that we can take along and cook on the trail."

"Ain't had no coffee for quite a spell," the old woman said sullenly, with a side glance at her husband. "Mister won't buy nothing but chicory—and it ain't fit for the hogs. Reckon I can fix you up with some of it—them other things, too, long as you're willing to pay."

"I've got hard money," Luther reassured her. "Be needing something to do the cooking in, along with the grub. Spider, lard bucket for the coffee, couple cups, plates, spoons and such."

"What about my team?" Oglesby cut in. "You want to buy it or not?"

"You come to a price yet?"

Oglesby narrowed an eye, scratched at his stained beard. "They're worth fifty dollars a piece."

"Fifty dollars!" Luther echoed. "That sure lets me out. How about renting—"

"Ain't renting nothing—"

"I'm a deputy sheriff," Luther said, producing his star. "I'm on important business. You'll get your horses back, along with proper pay soon as I—"

"Ain't renting nothing," Oglesby repeated stubbornly.

"You won't be losing nothing! I'm a lawman and I'll see to your getting paid—"

"Mister," Oglesby said, folding his arms and staring straight into Luther's face, "if you think I'm swallowing that hogwash, you're looney! I got you figured for a man on the run, and you're taking some jasper's wife with you —prob'ly talked her into running off with you. You lost your horses somewheres and now—"

"Take a good look at my star!" Luther shouted, thrusting it under the homesteader's nose. "Ought to be proof—"

"You could've bought that piece of tin. Man can do that about anywhere—"

"I've got papers—give me authority—"

"A man can get them, too, if he's of a mind. Just could be you killed a deputy somewhere, took his things off'n his dead body—"

"Oh, for hell's sake!" Luther exploded in disgust, and turned to the woman. "What about that grub and stuff? You going to fix us up or not?"

Callie glanced at her husband. He nodded, shrugged. She came back to Luther, said, "All right, I'll get a dollar's worth together for you. Be another dollar to the skillet and them other things you're wanting."

"Fine," Luther said, and started to follow the woman into the house. Oglesby lowered his weapon at once, barring the way.

"Just you do your waiting right where you are, mister. I want you where I can keep an eye on you."

Luther grinned. "Sure, sure. It all right if I fill my canteen at your well? Expect the lady could use a swallow or two of fresh water."

Oglesby thought for a moment, said, "Go ahead. Well's out back. You walk ahead of me—and don't try nothing."

"I'm not planning to," Luther said wearily. He had hoped to get the use of the horses from the man, had failed, and the prospect of more walking on the part of Nellie and himself was discouraging.

"You for certain you won't rent your horses to me?" he said, pausing. "I can leave you a deposit—"

"They ain't for rent, they're for sale," the homesteader snapped. "That's the only way you're getting them—buying them for fifty dollars a piece, else you can shut up about it."

"But we've got to have some way to reach the next

town, Mr. Oglesby," Nellie said in her most appealing way. "You can't expect us to walk—"

"Ain't expecting nothing 'cause it ain't none of my put-in," Oglesby said.

"Then maybe you'd let me stay here while the deputy goes for help. That way I'd be security for the loan of the horse."

Oglesby looked at Nellie Dupray dispassionately. "I ain't about to do no favor for any woman that's left her man for another'n."

"But I didn't!" Nellie cried. "It's just like he said—he's a deputy taking me to Capitol City and—"

"Here's your grub," Callie said, appearing in the back door. "Where's my two dollars?"

Luther stepped up to the old woman and took the two flour sacks she was holding.

"Where's the two dollars cash?" the woman repeated.

Luther shook his head. "I ain't trusting you no more'n you folks are trusting us," he said. "I aim to see what you've put in these sacks before I pay off."

Callie muttered something under her breath, stood by while he checked the contents of the bags. After a bit he looked up.

"Reckon there's two dollars worth there," he said, and producing the necessary coins, handed them to the woman.

Taking up the sacks, he tied the necks together in saddlebag fashion, and then crossed to the well, still under the hostile eyes of Oglesby. Emptying his canteen, he refilled it with fresh water, and then turning to Nellie, who was taking her fill from a tin dipper, handed the container to her.

"You'll be carrying this," he said. "I'll look after the grub."

Nellie hung the dipper back on its nail, shook her head. "I'm not carrying anything, Deputy—I'm staying right here. Sooner or later somebody'll come along, and I'll catch me a ride into—"

Luther, patience at an end, reached out, seized the woman by the arm and shook her roughly.

"Lady," he said in a grating voice. "I'm plumb sick and tired of talking to folks that're too dumb to pour water out of a boot—and I'm including you in on that. Now, you start walking north, toward them trees you can see over there, or I'm taking a switch to your hind end. You savvy?"

At once Nellie moved toward the edge of the yard. "Yes, I guess I do," she replied.

⚹ 12 ⚹

They reached the first of the trees, Nellie walking sullenly and silent a few steps in front of Luther. Darkness was now almost complete, and as they moved into the deep shadows of the grove, he looked back. Callie Oglesby was not to be seen but the old man, shotgun now cradled in his arms, was an indistinct figure observing their departure.

"We can pull up here," Luther said when he was certain they were no longer visible to the homesteader.

Nellie halted, turned to him. Hope filled her tired features. "Have you changed your mind? Are we going back to—"

"Just stopping here for a spell," Luther cut in.

The woman stiffened and her lips tightened with disappointment. After a moment she shook her head. "Well, I'm not taking one step farther, Deputy. You can mark that down in brass—"

"Seems I recollect you saying something like that before," Luther said mildly. "Still means nothing to me. We're going to Capitol City, and the pen. You can bet on it. I'll deliver you to that warden up there if I have to carry you all the way."

"That's what you'll have to do," Nellie said acidly. "I sure ain't walking!"

"Reckon you'll do what I tell you to," Luther said evenly. "Set down there on that log."

"Maybe I will—when I get ready—"

"Ma'am, you're sure heading for big trouble with me," Luther said grimly, and pivoting suddenly, he took the woman's shoulders in his big hands, lifted her off her feet and plumped her down solidly on the fallen tree trunk.

"Damn you—Deputy!" she shouted, jarred to the bone by his roughness. "I'll—"

"You ain't doing nothing but setting, lady," Luther said, and hanging the grub sacks on a clump of oak brush, he produced his handcuffs. Snapping one of the steel circles about her wrist, he locked the other about an ankle.

Bent forward due to the connecting chain's short length, light eyes blazing, Nellie glared at him.

"What are you doing this for? I—"

Luther had stepped to where he could see the Oglesby place through an opening in the trees. "Doing it because I don't trust you no farther'n I can throw a bull by the tail," he replied.

Nellie sniffed. "I wouldn't try to escape—"

"No, I expect you wouldn't—leastwise not until I was out of sight."

"Where could I go? I don't know where we are, or where there's a town—"

"That's right," he agreed, "but you'd likely find yourself a place and hide out—and I'm too dang tired to spend the rest of the night hunting you."

Nellie changed her position that she might better see

him in the near dark. "You talk like you're going somewhere."

"I'm getting us a couple of horses," Luther said in a flat, determined way. "Now, you keep quiet. You set up some kind of a ruckus and you'll sure do some walking—horse or not. I won't be gone long."

"But Oglesby said he wouldn't rent—" Nellie began and then hushed as the lawman, unheeding, melted into the shadows.

Luther walked hurriedly but quietly through the scattered clumps of brush, trying to remember if he'd seen a dog at Oglesby's. He couldn't recall having done so, and he doubted if there was one on the place; the crotchety old homesteader struck him as being a first rate penny-pincher and not of a mind to waste scraps on a pet.

Circling wide, he came in behind the barn with its adjoining corral. Earlier no horses had been in evidence so he was assuming they were inside the weathered structure. Halting at the side, he threw his glance to the house. Oglesby and his wife, a lamp between them, were sitting at a table in what apparently was the kitchen, having their evening meal. The homesteader likely would be thus occupied for a while. Wheeling, Luther moved to the rear of the barn, forced open the door, and entered.

It was pitch black inside the structure, rank with the smells of horses, wild hay, droppings and leather. Digging into his pockets for a match, he fired it. With the aid of its small flame, he located the runway and followed it to the horses.

Oglesby had three—or at least that was the number standing in the stalls near the front of the building. There appeared to be little difference in them, all being large farm animals suitable for pulling a plow or wagon. Accordingly, there being no choice, he backed the first two animals out into the runway and led them by their halters to the rear of the structure.

He had to have some light. Trying to find saddles and bridles and other necessary tack in the darkness of a strange barn and fitting them properly was out of the question. Leaving the horses tied near the door behind the shoulder high wall of the last stall, Luther doubled back forward. He found a lantern just inside the entrance to the place, started to retrace his steps—paused to have another look at the house. The Oglesbys were still at the table. Satisfied, he turned about, began to search for gear.

It required but a few minutes. Oglesby had a tack room at the lower end of the building. In it Luther found saddles, both old, one with the cantle broken; bridles, blankets—even another canteen. Taking his needs he returned to the horses, and with the aid of the lantern turned to its lowest point, made them ready for use. As he was completing the job he noted a woolen bed blanket draped over a rope line strung across an empty stall. Without hesitation he appropriated it also; Nellie would be needing it at night when the cold set in.

Finally finished, he reached into a pocket for the stub of pencil he carried, tore off the lower half of the letter of authority Sheriff Hollingshead had issued to him, and wrote a due-bill in the form of a note to Oglesby.

In it he explained that he truly was a deputy taking a prisoner to the penitentiary at Capitol City, that Indians had wrecked the stage on which they were traveling. He was sorry he had to borrow the two horses in the manner that he was doing, but it was necessary. They would be returned in good order, as would one wool blanket and the canteen, and suitable rent would be paid for their use. He signed the note Luther Pike, Deputy Sheriff, by authority of Sheriff Tom Hollingshead.

Looking about he located a prominently placed nail, affixed the note and hung the lantern. Oglesby, entering and seeing the light, would investigate immediately as a lantern burning inside the barn for no reason would strike him as being sheer waste.

That should satisfy the man, Luther believed. He'd tried to talk to him, make clear his dire need for the horses, but there'd been no reasoning with the homesteader, and borrowing them on the sly had been the only answer. And in handling the situation thus he was certain he'd have the approval of Sheriff Hollingshead. The lawman would understand the necessity for his actions since it was all in the line of duty.

Taking the reins of the two heavy-hoofed, barrel-bodied mounts in one hand, and carrying the blanket for Nellie in the other, Luther turned, headed for the rear door of the barn. Abruptly the wide, plank panel jerked open. Startled, Luther jumped back. It was Oglesby. In the dim light he could see that the homesteader again was holding a shotgun, had it leveled at him.

"Just what I allowed!" Oglesby said through clenched teeth. "A lousy, stinking horse thief—a dirty, thieving saddlebum—that's what you are!"

"Wait there just a damn minute!" Luther shouted back, suddenly angry with the way things were going. First the

Indians, and being forced to walk, the aggravation of
Nellie Dupray—and now this unreasonable, hide-bound,
narrow-minded, jug-headed homesteader! "I'm borrowing
these horses. Renting them—not stealing them. I put a
note right there on that nail, with the lantern. It's your receipt."

"Receipt ain't worth nothing to me!"

"That'n is! You'll get paid for me using your horses. I'm
a deputy—"

"You ain't nothing but a saddle tramp, like I done said
again and again, a'running away with some fellow's wife—
that's what you are! I've a mind to—"

"You're dead wrong, Oglesby," Luther said, striving to
keep his voice down. "That woman ain't nobody's wife.
She's my prisoner and I'm taking her to the pen, like I
keep trying to tell you. She's going to serve a long term
for rustling—"

"Rustling!" the homesteader echoed. "Now I know for
dang sure you're a dirty liar! Ain't never heard of no
woman rustler—and I misdoubt if anybody else ever has."

"Well, you're sure hearing about one now," Luther
stated, and taking another tack, he pointed at the weapon
in the homesteader's hands. "I'm ordering you to put
down that weapon and stand aside. You're interfering
with an officer of the law doing his duty!"

"I'm interfering with a thief stealing two of my horses,"
Oglesby countered. "Now, I'm ordering you—drop them
lines and step back!"

Luther, now simmering hotly, gave that brief consideration and shrugged. "You're making a mistake, mister."

"It's you making a mistake—thinking you could come sneaking in here, steal my horses and—"

Luther flung the old wool blanket he was taking back to Nellie straight at Oglesby. Half open, it spread over him like a smothering cloud. Head covered, arms impeded and unable to see, he staggered back. Luther sprang forward instantly and drove a balled fist into the area where he considered the homesteader's jaw would be.

Oglesby groaned, ceased his thrashing about and began to sink. Again quick, Luther reached out, seized the barrel of the shotgun outlined under the blanket, prevented its falling to the ground floor of the barn and perhaps going off on impact.

At once he pulled the blanket off the man and hung it over the saddle of the nearest horse. Then hurrying to the tack room where he had noticed a coil of rope, he returned, bound the unconscious man, gagged him with a bit of cloth that, unfortunately for Oglesby, smelled heavily of horse liniment, and then carrying the homesteader into the end stall, laid him out as comfortably as he could on the straw-littered floor.

Immediately Luther rejoined the horses, and mounting one, rode through the doorway with the other in tow. Oglesby's wife would soon miss her husband—unless she had retired and was now asleep—and come looking for him. Luther wanted to be as far from the place as possible when that occurred, which, if he was to judge by the speed he was getting out of the old blaze-faced, white stockinged bay he was astride, wouldn't be any considerable distance.

❈ 13 ❈

Nellie heard the thud of the horses' hooves, and hoping for the best and a bit of good luck, called out, "Help—over here! Please help me!"

In the next moment she sighed wearily in defeat as Luther rode into the small clearing and she recognized his dark outline. Dismounting, he stood for a long breath looking down at her. The stars had come out but their light was weak and he could not get a definite view of her face.

"You sure seem anxious to do a lot of walking," he said, dryly. "I told you not to try something."

She turned her head, met his gaze. "Deputy, I'll be trying something every foot of the way to the pen," she said coolly, and rattled the handcuffs. "I see you got the horses from Oglesby."

Luther produced his key, removed the manacles. Returning them to his pocket, he took up the sacks of grub, hung them, along with the wool blanket and canteens, across his saddle.

"I'm not saying he was much in favor of the idea," he said. "Fact is, we best get out of here fast. Way he looks at it I didn't borrow them, I stoled them."

"You—you just took them?" Nellie said in a disbelieving voice.

"I left him a receipt saying I'd return them and that he'd get paid for us using them, and I aim to keep my word. Only thing, I sort of had to knock him cold and tie him before I could leave. . . . You ride a horse?"

"Of course!" Nellie replied indignantly, and seized also by the need for urgency under the circumstances he had outlined, she bent forward, pulled her dress to waist high and secured it about her hips. Beneath it she was wearing a pair of ankle length pantaloons. "I'm ready."

Luther, in the process of tightening the cinch of his saddle, having found the battered old hull loose during the short trip from Oglesby's, glanced at her. Shock passed through him in a brief wave when he beheld the lace-trimmed undergarment, and then realizing the practicality of her act, nodded approvingly.

"Sure will make riding easier for you," he said, and turning to the horse she would be using, another bay marked much the same as his, led it up and assisted her to mount.

The stirrups were too long, but he was reluctant to spend time adjusting them, the feeling still strong within him that they had best get as far away from Oglesby's homestead as soon as possible.

"Put your feet in the loops," he said, doing it for her in the pale light. "Soon as we stop I'll fix them so's they'll fit."

"When are we stopping?" she asked at once. "I'm tired —and hungry."

"Be a few hours," Luther replied, and swinging up onto his saddle, he rode out of the clearing.

They traveled slowly but steadily until well past midnight, halting finally beside a water hole which was well off the trail that led north. He'd not make it easy for Oglesby, or anyone else the homesteader recruited, to follow him, Luther had earlier decided; while they lost a bit of ground by cutting away from the trail, he believed it was worthwhile.

Nellie was too exhausted to eat, and Luther felt much the same although he did munch a couple of the biscuits Callie Oglesby had put in the sack before he settled down in the brush a few paces from where the woman, wrapped in the wool blanket, had chosen to lie.

Worn, the weight of gradually accumulating responsibility riding his shoulders heavily, Luther did not immediately drop off to sleep despite weariness. For a time he lay quiet staring at the soft, black sky across which the stars had seemingly been flung so recklessly, and listening to the far off yapping of coyotes.

The horses stirred and stamped restlessly in their unfamiliar surroundings and on the yonder side of the water hole some small animal coming in to slake its thirst rattled the dry brush. The spring belonged to all the wild things, as well as the domesticated, and man; there would be many more furtive visitors during the night hours, Luther knew.

He found himself wishing the job was finished, that he'd completed the task of delivering Nellie Dupray to the warden—Slope the sheriff had called him—of the pen at Capitol City. He simply was not accustomed to responsibility of such magnitude and was finding it not only difficult to fulfill but contrary to his nature. The chore was far from over, however, in fact had only begun. He realized that, and realized, too, that if the woman could be believed, the worst was yet to come.

Her friends, whom she mentioned continually and always with the promise that they would put in their appearance eventually and in force and take her away from him, were waiting somewhere ahead. He had no reason to doubt that. Sheriff Hollingshead had warned him that Nellie had a host of friends all of whom would rally to the cause of freedom for her. Were all the tasks assigned to lawmen as difficult and ragging at the nerves as this one that he had been handed? Luther fell asleep, finally, pondering that question.

He awoke early and found Nellie up and moving quietly about. It struck him at once that she was attempting to steal away in the cool, half light with her horse, and make an escape. He wished he'd thought to bring along a bit of the rope he'd used to truss Oglesby—but he hadn't. It was no big problem, anyway; he'd take precautions with other means the next time they halted for the night.

Feigning unawareness of the woman's activity, Luther rose, noisily made the fact known and began making preparations for breakfast. Nellie at once abandoned her covert movements and turned to assist him.

They made a meal of warmed over biscuits, dried meat and chicory, and set out, again riding northward but avoiding the customary trail. Nellie was in much better spirits, apparently visualizing the possibility of an escape during the coming night—or believing that help from her friends was not too distant now that they were on the final leg of the journey.

Around noon, with the sun once more streaming down on them with fierce intensity, they halted beneath a solitary tree on the crest of a hill to rest the horses. Off to their right a mile or so the irregular blur of a settlement sprawled in a hollow could be seen. Nellie, fanning herself with a leafed twig broken off a low branch, stared at it longingly.

"We could spend the night there, Deputy, get us a good meal, sleep in a bed," she suggested. "I wouldn't mind us being in the same room—if you were scared to let me stay alone. Oh, it would be so good to be comfortable again—be clean—"

"Forget it," Luther said bluntly. "We're not going near no town—not that one or any other."

Nellie pouted prettily. "Why not? What would it hurt?"

"There's bound to be some of your friends there, that's why. Maybe not the ones you're expecting to show up, but some that would try taking you away from me. I'd sure hate to kill a man trying that."

Nellie snickered. "You kill a man?" she jeered, pointing at the old pistol hanging at his side. "I doubt if you'd ever get up enough sand to use that thing."

Luther shrugged. "I reckon I could if I had to," he said.

"Friends of mine are all gunmen, fast on the draw. And I've seen some of them shoot the neck off a whiskey bottle from clear across a street—"

"Yeh, I expect they're real good at things like that," he

said indifferently, his attention on a bristly black and gray badger squirming his way along the edge of the brush at the foot of the ridge. "We best get going."

Nellie arose reluctantly, gazed again on the distant town. "If I gave you my word there'd be no trouble, could we go there and—"

"Nope," Luther cut in flatly, and taking her by the elbow, he escorted her to her horse and all but boosted her onto the saddle.

He heard her swearing quietly at him as he turned to his own mount and swung aboard. He was frowning as he faced her.

"Sure don't appreciate your cussing at me—not that it ain't been done before, but other times I maybe had it coming. That ain't the way of it here. I don't like what I'm doing any more'n you do—and I'm liking it less and less. It sure ain't what I bargained for when I made up my mind I wanted to be a lawman."

"Then why not chuck it right here and now?" Nellie said eagerly. "I'll make it worth plenty to you."

Luther studied her soberly from the broad back of the old bay, standing patiently in the driving sunlight.

"You saying you'd pay me to let you go?"

"Exactly! You get me to one of the towns where I'm known—there's a lot of them west of here—and I'll raise enough cash to—"

"Nope, I reckon not," Luther said, halting her hurried flow of words. "I'm maybe sick of this here job, and getting sicker, but I'll finish it. I never was no hand to quit . . . move out."

They rode on, Nellie in glum silence, Luther equally

thoughtful. The hush between them held until darkness began to close in and the need to find a suitable place for night camp presented itself. They were in an area of low, wooded hills, and Luther could see no indication of a spring or stream anywhere although he had watched throughout the last hour of daylight. He guessed they'd get by, however; both canteens were near full, and that should carry them through to the next water hole.

"Pull up over there in them cedars," he directed, pointing to a stand of the thick, squat trees. "About the best place we're going to find around here."

Nellie gave him no response, simply guiding her horse toward the spot indicated. Reaching there she halted. Luther, pulling up beside her, stiffened suddenly. Alarm spurted through him. A shifting of the slight breeze had brought the smell of smoke.

"Turn around—we're heading back out—" he began, and broke off as a man stepped out of the trees, facing them.

"Well, if it ain't Nellie Dupray!" he said, grinning widely. "What're you doing out here in the hills?"

✄ 14 ✄

Luther's first impulse was to draw his pistol. Additional motion among the cedars to the left and right stayed him. Shortly three more men, all dressed in the range clothing of cowhands—sturdy pants, boots, coarse shirts, bandannas and wide-brimmed hats—moved into view. Each was armed, as could be expected, and all were slightly drunk.

Nellie beamed. "Well, if it ain't Kirk Beasley! I might ask you the same—what are you doing here?"

"Me and my buddies are headed for Matamoros. Got us jobs down there . . . You know them?"

The woman shook her head. Beasley, somewhere in his middle twenties, as were his friends, gestured at them.

"Short one there's called Sugar. Nate Carson's the skinny jasper. Barney Aiken's the one with all the whiskers. Boys, this here's Nellie Dupray. Knowed her from Silver City. Now, if you're ever honing to have yourself a big time—and you've got the money—you just look old Nellie up."

The cowhands all grinned. Barney Aiken doffed his stained hat, bowed sheepishly, said, "Ma'am, why'nt you and your friend there come on into camp. It's just back of these trees. We're fixing to eat."

"That's right," Beasley said. "Heard your horses coming, figured we'd best play it cozy 'til we seen who it was."

Nellie nodded, and smiling coyly at Luther, allowed Beasley to take the headstall of her horse's bridle in his hand and start back through the scatter of trees. Luther followed, thankful that he'd had sense enough not to go for his gun. So far he still had it—which would not have been the case had he attempted to draw it.

With Sugar and the others trailing along and all the while eyeing wonderingly the two lumbering plow horses, they moved deeper into the grove and came to a halt finally in a small open area. In its center a fire was going and over it was suspended a kettle containing a stew of some sort. Nearby a blackened coffee pot was issuing a white stream of steam, its lid rattling softly, while off a short distance the cowhands' four mounts grazed on the thin grass.

Beasley made a wide sweeping gesture, grinned. "It ain't much, but it's home," he said jokingly and helped Nellie off her saddle.

Nate Carson, rocking back on his heels, thumbs hooked in his belt, stared at the woman's pantaloons. "I sure do admire them fancy chaps you're wearing," he said.

Nellie tossed her head, shook down her dress. "You ought to see the ones I wear on Sundays!" she shot back.

Luther, coming off his horse, felt the attention of the men shift expectantly to him. Beasley thrust out his hand.

"We ain't been introduced, friend, but I sure like the kind of traveling partner you pick. Nellie's a real dandy to be with."

"Maybe he's a friend of yours, but he sure ain't one of mine," Nellie said, crossing to stand well away from Luther.

Beasley, pulling a near empty pint bottle of whiskey from a hip pocket, frowned, glanced at her. "He ain't? Then what're you—"

"He's a lawman—a deputy sheriff. He's taking me to the pen up at Capitol City—or's figuring to."

Complete silence claimed Beasley and the others for a long breath, and then the one called Sugar, weaving slightly on his feet, whistled quietly.

"Well, now, don't that skin the possum for you!" he said.

"The pen?" Beasley repeated. "What's he doing that for?"

"Yeh," Nate Carson added, his voice a bit thick, "what'd you do to buy yourself some time in the calaboose?"

"Jury down Linksburg way claimed I was in on some cattle rustling," Nellie explained. "Was three jaspers I knew doing that all right, but I wasn't nothing but a good friend to a couple of them. It was because of that I got rung in on the charges. Ended up with them getting hung and me going to the pen for life."

"Now, that's a danged shame," Sugar said, and drew his pistol. "Ain't that what you all say, boys?"

Beasley and the others sounded quick agreement. Sugar cocked the weapon, the clack of the hammer coming back loud in the hush.

"Locking up a fine woman like you'd sure be a waste—

if you're all Kirk there claims, and I expect you are. I don't reckon we ought to allow it—do you, boys?"

Again there was total agreement. Beasley rubbed at the stubble on his jaw, listened briefly to the distant moaning of a dove, and then faced the woman.

"How about it, Nellie? You want to string along with us? Can drop you off anywhere you say—or maybe you'd as soon go on with us to Matamoros."

"Any chance of you swinging by San Antone?" she asked.

"Hell, yes! Couple, three more days ain't going to make no difference to us."

"No, ma'am, it sure won't," Sugar said, eyeing the woman. "Can take all the time we want. Jobs'll still be waiting."

"What about the deputy?" Aiken, the nearest to being sober, asked. "You're kind of forgetting him, ain't you?"

Beasley glanced at Luther. "Well, what about him? We'll just dehorn him and ride off with Nellie."

"Taking his gun ain't going to keep him from high-tailing it to the nearest town and setting the law on us. Losing a prisoner is something that riles them a'plenty."

Beasley again scrubbed at his jaw. "We could set him a'foot—"

"Appears to me he's just about in that shape now," Aiken said, studying the old bay Luther was riding. "The law must be mighty hard up, putting you two to riding a couple of crow-baits like them."

"He stole them from a homesteader down the way," Nellie said. "We started out aboard the stage, ended up walking when some Indians wrecked it. Then we—"

"Why don't we just put a bullet in his head?" Sugar suggested, ignoring Nellie's words. "That sure'n hell keep him quiet."

Luther took a step forward. It was time he made a strong stand, let them know the law was not to be trifled with.

"I'm warning you," he said coldly, "you're interfering with the law—with a lawman doing his duty. I'm telling you right now to back off—don't go mixing in!"

"You're telling us?" Beasley said, laughing. "Deputy, in case you can't count there's four of us to one of you—five adding in Nellie, and I've seen the day when she was good as any man! It's us that's going to do all the telling—you best savvy that. Get his gun, Barney."

Aiken nodded, started toward the lawman. A surge of anger swept through Luther.

"I'm warning you again!" he shouted, leveling a long finger at the cowhand. "Don't go meddling with me!"

Barney Aiken grinned, closed in. Luther's jaw tightened, showed white at the corners. If the odds against him hadn't been so overwhelming, and getting his prisoner delivered so important, it's unlikely he would have elected to inflict such cruel punishment on any man. But the situation was critical and, as Barney Aiken reached out, Luther brought his booted foot up, drove the toe deep and hard into the man's crotch.

Aiken howled in pain, buckled forward. Instantly Luther whipped out his pistol. Sugar already had his weapon in hand, trying to pull aside and get off a shot without hitting the reeling Barney Aiken. Luther faced no such obstacle. He fired, and the bullet struck Sugar in the leg, knocking him to the ground. Beasley and Nate Carson, seemingly paralyzed, stood frozen.

"Anybody else want to try me?" Luther demanded, thoroughly aroused. Legs spread, hunched, sweat glistening on his face, he was in no mood to brook further opposition. "Go on—one of you—both of you—pull your guns! I'll shoot you both dead!"

Kirk Beasley and Carson only stared, gaze wandering from the writhing Barney Aiken, now also prone on the ground, to Sugar, clutching his bleeding leg and moaning a stride or two from them. Luther motioned to Nellie with his pistol.

"Climb on your horse," he ordered, curtly. "We're getting out of here."

He waited until the woman had rolled up her skirt once again and pulled herself onto the saddle. Then, moving to Aiken, he relieved him of his weapon, and tossed it off into the brush. That done, he followed the same procedure with the other cowhands until all had been disarmed, after which he swung onto his own mount.

"Don't you fret none, Nellie," Beasley called out as Luther, riding close behind the woman, left the camp. "We'll be catching up and—"

Luther pulled his horse to an abrupt stop. He leveled his pistol at the man. "You ain't following one single step, mister!" he said in a promising sort of voice. "You do and you're dead because I'll be watching and waiting for you."

Beasley swallowed noisily and glanced about. Carson, standing beside him, pulled away as if taking care to not be in the line of fire should the lawman decide to not hold off but start shooting immediately. Aiken was now sitting up but showed no interest in the world beyond his own personal pain. Sugar, however, still lay groaning on the ground.

"I make myself plain?" Luther pressed.

There was no response from Kirk Beasley for several moments and then, shoulders going down, he nodded.

"Yeh, reckon you do," he said, and switched his eyes to the woman. "I'm sure sorry, Nellie, but this here deputy's got us by the short hair. There just ain't nothing we can do."

"Oh, go to hell!" she said in a voice filled with disgust, and kicking at the flanks of her horse, moved off into the gathering darkness.

Luther, with a last warning glance at the cowhands, sighed inwardly and followed. Out of sight he holstered his pistol and brushed at the sweat on his forehead. It seemed to him his glory road was getting mighty rough.

✻ 15 ✻

Caution had quickly become second nature to Luther since embarking upon a career as a lawman. Where heretofore, he'd given little thought to the future, and the possibility of its non-existence, he now found himself seriously considering all probabilities.

Kirk Beasley and his friends were not likely to accept the defeat he had dealt them—not when the spoils of war was Nellie Dupray. Even the wounded Sugar, who just might be forced to ride side-saddle in deference to the bullet hole in his leg, would undoubtedly join in the pursuit and search as soon as they could get themselves organized. Thus he felt it was necessary that they continue on through the darkness, sick as he was of the game of hide-and-seek he was being compelled to play across a land so barren in places at times that it was far from easy.

"We keep going 'til midnight," he informed Nellie gruffly as they rode slowly on aboard Oglesby's plodding plow horses. "And keep cutting to the left. Less chance of your friends finding us on those hills."

Nellie murmured something and drew her blanket closer about her shoulders. Sunset had brought a halt to the driving heat, but now, only a few hours past, a chill had set in. It was not unexpected by Luther; he knew it to be a country where the elements never went half way. It was either hot or cold, bone dry or sopping wet, leaving a man to forever cope with extremes.

They halted under the overhang of a low bluff at the appointed time, and Nellie again declaring herself too weary to eat, rolled up in the blanket and immediately went to sleep.

Luther, first doing what he could for the tired horses, had himself a bite or two, washed it down with water, and then selecting a spot where he had a good view of the slope below, also settled down for the remainder of the night.

Beasley and his friends, apparently deciding that bracing Luther and his pistol for Nellie wasn't worth the price, failed to show, and that next morning after a quick breakfast, they were again in the saddle and working steadily northward.

That day and the one succeeding passed with monotonous similarity, both filled with endless flats and hills, blistering heat, dust, and ceaseless, aggravating wind. Night, never so welcome, found them at the edge of a small creek, one well shaded by several cottonwood trees and not too far from a settlement. In the fading sunlight it looked to be of fair size.

Nellie, sliding wearily off her saddle, stared longingly at the distant blur with its several twisting smoke columns. After a bit she turned to Luther, who was casting about for a suitable place to picket the horses. For a change they would enjoy good grazing.

"Deputy, can't we go to that town—spend the night there?"

Luther paused, glared at her. "You going to start that again?"

"I'll give you my promise—my word—"

"I already told you your word ain't worth nothing to me. I've had a sample of what happens when some friends of yours comes along."

"But I really mean it! I'm so tired and hungry for a decent meal—and I need a bath so bad—"

"Can take one right here in the creek when I get back," Luther said, digging into a hip pocket. "Got to fetch us some groceries. About to run out."

Nellie perked up immediately. "You're riding over to that town?"

"Now, where the hell do you think I'd be going for grub?" he demanded testily. As worn as the woman from lack of sleep and the constant, slow traveling, Luther was finding himself on edge continually—a state of mind he, heretofore, had lapsed into. "Give me your hand. I'm cuffing you—"

Nellie jerked away. Luther lunged forward, caught her by the arm and swung her roughly toward a flat rock near the stream and sat her down upon it with jarring force. Snapping on the cuffs, wrist to ankle, as before, he stepped back, looked down at her in the failing light.

"About time you learned I ain't of a mind to fool around with you."

"You ain't got a mind," Nellie observed coolly, and lay back on the grass.

Luther grinned crookedly. "Maybe not, but it's me taking you to jail, not the other way around." Swinging up onto his horse, he headed for the settlement.

The name of the town was Anson. It seemed busy as Luther turned onto its single main street and angled for the first general store that caught his eye. Such activity was all in his favor, he felt; he'd not draw the attention strangers ordinarily did.

Entering the store he made his purchases from a man wearing, along with other things, a bib apron and black sateen sleeve guards—and who never relinquished for a moment the corncob pipe clenched between his broad teeth.

Needs fulfilled, Luther returned to his horse, hung the sack of provisions on the saddle, and noting the Yellow-jacket Saloon immediately adjacent, decided to treat himself to a couple of beers. He also bought a bottle of whiskey, the thought being that if Nellie had a drink now and then she, perhaps, might be easier to manage.

The beer downed, the bourbon, or what passed for such, under his arm, Luther doubled back to the street. The fading sunlight, mellow gold in its last stages, had softened the harsh, bleached lines of the settlement, and for a time he stood on the narrow porch of the saloon letting the town register on his consciousness.

A bit down the way he spotted Green's Restaurant—Home-Cooked Meals; and on beyond it stood, at two-storied level, the Canyon Hotel. From outside appearances the latter looked to be somewhat rundown but, as weary of makeshift trail camps as Nellie, even the worst would be a welcome change.

A good meal of steak, potatoes and hot biscuits, a bed under a roof with a carpet for a man's bare feet—a pitcher of water and a bowl to wash in—all had risen to the category of luxuries. But they weren't for him. He had too much responsibility riding on his shoulders, and because of that responsibility—in the form of Nellie Dupray—he'd have to do his sleeping out on the cold, hard ground and stomach his own cooking which, as Percy Gilmore took great pains to tell everybody interested, sure wasn't much.

Nellie was dozing, or playing at it, when he returned to the camp. Ignoring her, he unloaded the horse, picketed it along with the other bay and set about putting a meal together. They would eat well that evening, he had decided on the way back—go all out, in fact. He'd thin slice some potatoes, fry the meat, heat bread, open a can of peaches, make real coffee instead of using some of the chicory Callie Oglesby had provided, and top it all off with the dried apple pie he'd found at the general store.

Nellie stirred into wakefulness as he set to work, and pausing to remove the cuffs, he waved her toward the stream.

"You can be taking that bath you're wanting while I fix supper."

She rubbed at her ankle and wrist, relieving the chafing. "Not sure I want to now," she murmured. "Water looks cold—and there's no towel."

"Suit yourself," Luther replied indifferently. "Just don't go wandering off. I want you in sight all the time."

Nellie looked at him smilingly. "Even when I'm taking a bath?"

He did not bother to glance up. "Even then."

Nellie frowned, studied him narrowly. "Maybe you're

more man than I figured," she said, and rising, moved off to the creek.

Luther watched until she had stopped at the edge of a stand of willows, growing partly in the water, and there began to remove her clothing. At that point he resumed his preparations for the meal; Nellie wasn't likely to run off.

The supper turned out to be most enjoyable, possibly because Luther had taken time and considerable trouble —and perhaps due, also, to the fact that they both were hungry. When it was over and they were beside the low fire drinking coffee, Luther remembered the whiskey. Rising, he obtained the bottle from his saddlebags, and returning to where Nellie, propped on an elbow, lay on her blanket staring vacantly into the flames, he pulled the cork and offered it to her.

Taking the bottle by the neck, Nellie sat up slowly, frowning. Full dark had long since settled in and the only light now was from the stars and the small fire. In its flickering glow, her features were soft, almost lovely.

"Figured you might like a drink now and then," Luther said, resuming his place.

Nellie's mouth had tightened. "You did—did you!" she snapped, suddenly angry. Raising her arm, she threw the bottle off into the brush.

Luther stiffened in surprise. "Now, why'd you do that?" he demanded.

"Why?" Nellie echoed. "I'll tell you why! If you think you're going to get me drunk—soften me up so's you can—"

"I ain't thinking no such a damn thing!" Luther shouted indignantly. "I wasn't about to even—"

"I suppose I'm not good enough for you, being a saloon woman—and a criminal—"

Luther swore in exasperation. "No—no such a thing—ma'am! You're a fine looker and I'd be proud to, well, do what you're saying—but it just wouldn't be right! I'm a lawman and you're my prisoner, so it'd not be fitting and proper—even if we had the time—"

"We've got the time—all night—but far as I'm concerned you can forget it."

"I don't need to forget, 'cause I wasn't figuring on it in the first place," Luther said wearily, and rising walked off toward the stand of brush into which Nellie had thrown the bottle.

Poking about in the half dark he found it, finally, lying on its side in a bush, tipped, and with still a few swallows trapped inside. Raising it to his lips, he drained it. The raw liquor gagged him slightly, but it was good, brought a flow of warmness coursing through him that dulled the edge of his troubles.

Moving a few steps farther along the stream, he stood for a bit thinking about the changes that had entered his life since becoming a lawman. Some, admittedly, weren't good. And he wondered, too, if being a lawman was going to be all he was expecting it to be. One thing for damn sure, he was finding out, it was no easy job.

But then he could just be undergoing a sort of test, he reasoned. It could be that Sheriff Hollingshead purposely assigned him the difficult task of escorting Nellie Dupray to the pen knowing all along that it would be a job to tax his courage and resourcefulness—not to mention patience. Nellie had claimed Hollingshead had done just that, but for different reasons—none of which had made any sense to him.

Tom Hollingshead was a big-time lawman; he'd not be afraid to take on the chore of delivering a woman, regardless of who she might be, to the penitentiary; neither would Chief Deputy Herb Slocum. It was simply, as the sheriff had explained, that both he and Slocum were tied up, and he was the only deputy available. That, when he mulled it about in his mind, sounded more reasonable than it being a test.

But if he had his choosings, Luther reckoned he'd rather have started off his career as a lawman at something less demanding, less wearing on the nerves—maybe even a mite less dangerous. On the other hand, however, he supposed it was just as well he got the worst over with —like taking a dose of ipecac; best to gulp it down fast, have done with it.

He reckoned he'd live through it, if he kept his eyes and ears open and his wits about him—which was what really counted. And then after he got Nellie delivered to the warden and had a receipt for her in his pocket ready to hand over to Tom Hollingshead, he would have proved he was made of the stuff that being a good lawman requires. Too, if the sheriff had for the reasons Nellie set forth, deliberately laid the job of escorting her to Capitol City and the nearby pen because he feared failure, then he would have the last laugh.

Luther glanced up at the sky, noted the fewer stars due to a gathering overcast, and pivoting started back to the camp. A light shower would cool things off a bit, and that would certainly be welcome. Walking slowly, he looked ahead.

Nellie was still sitting on the blanket by the fire, now blazing up brightly from added fuel. He would as soon she hadn't thrown on more wood; the glare could attract someone. Drawing up beside it, he kicked off several branches to lower the flames.

"No sense letting the whole country know where we are," he said, studying her thoughtfully. "Or was you doing that a'purpose?"

The woman shrugged, reached for the corners of the wool blanket and drew it about her shoulders. "Never came to my mind, but it's an idea. Maybe I'll try it later on."

"And maybe I'd just better handcuff you to that tree behind you," Luther shot back, angrily. "I—"

"Now, that sure ain't no way to talk to a lady, mister," a voice said from the shadows ringing the fire.

❈ 16 ❈

Luther froze. His hand, moving almost imperceptibly, drifted toward the pistol on his hip.

"That's enough of that!" the voice in the shadows warned. "You make one more move to draw that iron and me and my bunkie'll blow your guts all over the slope!"

Luther nodded slightly indicating his complete understanding, and arms hanging stiffly at his sides, stared at the pocket of darkness from which the voice had come. Nellie, too, had turned her attention to that point. Two figures, both in dirty, torn army uniforms, emerged, eased slowly up the edge of the fire's flare.

One, a small, wiry, dark man halted abruptly, eyes fixed on the woman. His jaw sagged, and then he grinned widely.

"Well, if it ain't Nellie Dupray! Sure never figured to run into you way up here!"

Nellie got to her feet, gaze on the soldier. "Not sure I remember—"

"The hell you say! I'm Travis McGee!"

"Travis—from down around El Paso—Fort Bliss."

"Right! You was working in Bertie Grimshaw's house, along the river."

Nellie said, "That's right. Good old Bertie. Who's your friend?"

Luther swore soundlessly. Another member of Nellie's far-flung circle of acquaintances. He wondered if there was any place in the entire country where she'd encounter someone she didn't know—or who didn't know her.

"Keeter Perkins," McGee said, glancing around as if to make certain there was no one else present. "Me and him just went over the hill."

"Deserted!" Nellie exclaimed in a disapproving voice. "Hell, Travis, you know you won't get away with it. They'll catch you sure."

"I'm willing to take my chances," Perkins said, speaking up. He was somewhat taller and younger than McGee, had bulky, cotton hair and a round, boyish face. "I sure've had all that guard house I'm wanting."

Nellie shook her head, and bending over took up a handful of branches and tossed them onto the dwindling fire.

"You mean you were in the stockade?" she said.

"Just where we were," McGee replied, jovially. "Can't blame us for busting out. We'd been in there about three months."

"Had to stove in the corporal of the guard's head doing it, but—"

"Never mind, Keeter," McGee cut in. "Best we don't talk too much about some things." The deserter paused, jerked a thumb at Luther. "What's this jasper up to—talking about handcuffing you to a tree? What's going on, Nellie?"

"He's a deputy sheriff, name's Luther Pike," she answered. "He's taking me to Capitol City, turning me over to the warden at the pen."

"You're going to jail?"

"Seems I am—"

"What in the hell for?"

"Rustling! Can you believe that? Only thing I ever rustled was an extra dollar out of some jaybird's pants pocket when he wasn't looking."

"Best you hear it all," Luther said, breaking silence. "She was convicted by a jury and sentenced by a judge. Three men that were in it with her got hung. I'm warning you not to interfere with—"

"Hold your tongue, Deputy!" McGee snapped, and keeping his pistol leveled at Luther, he squatted, gathered up more dry branches and tossed them onto the fire. As the flames soared brightly, he considered the lawman with a critical eye.

"You sure'n hell don't look like no deputy I've ever seen," he declared. "Was I guessing about you I'd say you was some saddlebum with maybe half enough sense to pull cockleburs out of a horse's tail."

Luther stiffened angrily, and the corner of his jaw whitened. "What you guess—"

"His first time on the job," Nellie broke in with a laugh. "I'm the only prisoner he's ever had to look after."

Keeter Perkins was staring at the spider, resting on the rocks at the edge of the fire. There was still an amount of browned potatoes and meat left in it, along with several biscuits that were also left over. The tin of coffee, however, was almost empty.

"I'm sure hungry," the young soldier said.

"Then you just help yourself!" McGee invited. "It'll be all right with Nellie—and we ain't givin' a hoot to what the deputy thinks." A moment later he added, apparently as an afterthought, "Save me a couple of bites, boy."

"Sure, sure," Perkins replied. Stepping forward, he began to dig into the food with his fingers. After a few mouthfuls, he reached for Luther's canteen, poured a quantity of water into the lard tin and placed it over the flames. Nodding to McGee he said, "Coffee'll be ready right soon, Sarge."

Nellie smiled. "Sergeant, eh! You've come up in the ranks since I last saw you, Travis. You were a buck private then."

"Come up and gone down, like a monkey on a string," McGee said, ruefully. "Got busted and my stripes took more'n a year ago. Keefer can't get out of the habit of calling me Sarge."

Perkins, his estimation of a fair portion of food bolted down, rose, and taking the pistol from McGee, passed the skillet to the older man. Wiping his mouth with the back of a hand, he nodded.

"Here you go, Sarge—it's mighty fine eating. You go right ahead and feed your face. I'll keep an eye on this john-law 'til you're done . . . coffee ain't boiled yet."

McGee made the exchange, and quickly cleaning out the remainder of food in the pan, glanced around. "You got a drink handy, Nellie?" he asked, dropping the skillet near the fire. "I could sure use one."

"Water and coffee, best I can do," she answered. "Where you boys headed?"

Back in the trees an owl hooted forlornly. An alertness

came over McGee, and for a long breath he was motionless. Finally, he shrugged, grinned.

"Reckon that was a danged owl all right. Fighting redskins and listening to them signal back and forth kind of makes you suspicious. What'd you say?"

"Asked you where were you going—"

"West—to California," McGee said, reclaiming his pistol from Keeter Perkins. Gesturing at Luther again with a thumb, he continued, "Help yourself to the deputy's iron there, boy. Best you take belt and all. We'll be needing them bullets . . . Nellie, you want to come along with us? You're sure welcome."

Rigid, Luther allowed the grinning Keeter to unbuckle his belt, and take possession of his pistol, holster and near-full cartridge belt. His eyes were on McGee, however; Travis was the dangerous one, and unfortunately, it was he who was holding a gun on him. If it had been the reverse and it was Perkins leveling the weapon at him, he would have been inclined to chance it, make some sort of move to overcome the pair. Keeter appeared to be a bit on the addled side.

But that wasn't the way of it, and with anger now welling through him at high tide, Luther stood motionless while submitting to the ignobility of being disarmed.

"You'd better listen to me!" he said, suddenly, unable to remain silent. "You're interfering with the law! This can get you in a powerful lot of trouble!"

McGee laughed. "Just what do you think we're in now, Deputy? We ain't playing no game for fun—we're playing for keeps. If we don't make it and get caught—we're dead. There'll be a firing squad waiting for us. The kind of trouble you can cause ain't even penny-ante stuff far as the army's concerned."

He hesitated, glanced at Perkins, saw that he had managed to strap on Luther's gun, and was now admiring himself.

"Keeter, go bring up the horses. We best be moving right along—the post ain't far enough away yet to suit me."

"Yes, sir, Sarge," Perkins said, and shambled off into the darkness.

Luther drew to attention as his hopes lifted. The opportunity just might present itself now to turn matters around—with Keeter Perkins off in the night and McGee plainly a bit on the anxious and nervous side.

"Which one of them nags is yours?" he heard McGee ask Nellie.

"One there by the rocks—not that it makes any difference. Can go faster walking—it just ain't as tiresome when you're riding."

"I got me a pretty fair horse," McGee said, "but I dassen't try riding double. Just might have to make a run for it, and loaded down with two people, he'd likely peter out."

"I understand—"

"And if me and Keeter have to run for it, could be I'll have to leave you behind, Nellie. That be all right with you?"

She shrugged. "Sure. Just get me loose of the deputy there, that's all I'm asking." Nellie paused, then, "He's got some papers about me in his pocket—supposed to be handed over to the warden. Expect I'd better get them, throw them in the fire. As soon nobody'd ever see them."

The woman turned, crossing to where Luther was standing. Tense, he watched her move up, noting McGee following behind but keeping his distance.

"I want the papers, Deputy," Nellie said, halting before him and extending her hand.

"Help yourself," Luther said indifferently. "I ain't about to make a move that'd get me shot by the sergeant there."

"Go ahead," McGee said dryly. "It's what you're getting anyway."

"Just whatever you say," Luther said, and raising his arms, seized Nellie by the shoulders and threw her directly into the man.

Nellie screamed. McGee, cursing wildly, went stumbling backward into the fire. As he tripped over the rocks and went down the pistol in his hand fired, sending a bullet streaking up into the night's dark sky. In the next instant Luther was upon him, had wrenched the weapon from his grasp and clubbed the deserter into unconsciousness.

Grim, jaw set, anger still throbbing through him, and ignoring Nellie sprawled full length on the ground, gasping for breath, he dragged the limp McGee out of the fire and into the shadows.

"Sarge?"

Keeter Perkin's voice raised questioningly came almost too quickly for Luther. Fading into the darkness, he circled the camp to get in behind the deserting soldier.

"What'd you do—shoot that there deputy?"

"Look out—Keeter!" Nellie shouted her warning. "He's—"

Her words were too late. Luther, in back of Perkins, lunged from the shadows, threw his weight solidly against the younger, lighter man. As Keeter staggered, off balance, Luther clubbed him hard with Travis McGee's gun, driving him to the ground.

Breathing heavily, Luther straightened up, his anger and frustration again having their way with him. There was nothing but trouble—nothing but somebody horning in doing their best to block his road, making it impossible for him to get his job done! Damn it all anyway—was everybody in the country down on lawmen?

Reaching down, he retrieved his belt and gun from Keeter and strapped it on. Then, taking the unconscious soldier by the collar, he moved him over beside McGee. Nellie had recovered her wind. She was now getting to her feet, pure hatred glowing in her eyes as she dusted herself off.

"Get ready," he ordered. "We're pulling out."

"I ain't taking one solitary step—" she began stubbornly and then quailed as he pivoted, striding purposefully toward her. "All right, all right, Deputy," she added hastily, extending her hands palms outward to him as if to ward off a blow. "I'll come along. Won't make no difference, anyway. My friends'll be showing up soon now."

Luther shrugged wearily. "Expect they will," he said. "Ain't nothing gone right for me yet on this job."

❊ 17 ❊

Luther had left McGee and Keeter Perkins tied to each other with rope he had found on one of their saddles. Both were still unconscious thanks to an additional tap or two on the head. He had also taken possession of McGee's pistol, and appropriated their horses, assuring Nellie that leaving them afoot would pose no serious problem since they could make their way to Anson, only a short distance to the east. Nellie had merely sniffed, making it clear that their welfare was of no interest to her.

Now, astride more suitable saddle horses, and leading the pair belonging to Oglesby, they rode on through the night. It was becoming a habit, Luther thought, this halting at sundown, making camp and then moving on for some reason to finally settle down around midnight for sleep and rest. To say the least the odd schedule was beginning to catch up with him.

Accustomed to crawling into his blanket at a much earlier hour and on a regular basis, except perhaps for one night a week—Saturday—when he went to town with Percy Gilmore and maybe some of the other hands to shoot pool and have a few beers, the change being forced upon him was not being well accepted.

But he took it all as an unusual and not customary

phase in the career he'd undertaken, and promised himself that it would soon be over—assuming he was able to
live through the next few days and nights—and he could
get himself and his living habits back on a sensible time-
table.

They stopped at the usual hour, around twelve o'clock,
and made camp. Both were awake shortly after dawn,
had a good breakfast and again continued on their way.
Traveling was much easier on the mounts taken from the
two deserters, but since they were leading the pair bor-
rowed from Oglesby, progress was only a little faster.

"What are you planning to do with them?" Nellie
asked, impatiently. It was around mid-morning. The sky
had cleared leaving an open blue field for the sun, and
the day was already burning hot. "Why don't you just
turn them loose—we'd make a lot better time."

"And get hung for horse stealing?" Luther said. "No,
ma'am, I'm taking them back to Oglesby just as soon as I
hand you over to that warden at the pen."

"What about the ones we're riding? The army'll be
after you for stealing them—and I don't think they deal
with horse thieves any kinder than does the law."

"They're not the army's," Luther said. "No U.S. brand
on them—and army always brands its animals. Them deserter friends of yours must've stole them from some
rancher."

"Then you'll have some rancher out looking for them—
and you—"

"Could be," Luther said, mopping at the sweat on his
forehead. "I'm hoping we get to Capitol City before that

happens. Can turn them over to the sheriff there, ask him to get them back to whoever owns them."

"And could be whoever that is will turn up before we get there—"

"Reckon I'll just have to explain how we come to be riding them. Ain't much else I can do."

Nellie smiled, dabbing at her face with the ends of her scarf. "Sure wish you luck, Deputy," she said, dryly. "Happens I know a little about rustling. They don't listen to nothing—anything you try to tell them. They just go by what they see, and start throwing a rope over the nearest tree limb."

"Little different, me being a lawman."

"You're fooling yourself. It won't make no difference at all . . . How far are we from Capitol City?"

"Couple of days, I figure. Ain't sure. Why? You fretting some because them friends of yours ain't shown up yet?"

"Nope, they'll come," Nellie replied coolly. "Can lay odds on it."

Luther patted the pistol in his holster and then the one taken from Travis McGee, tucked under his belt.

"They can come any time they take the notion. I'll be ready for them."

This time Nellie didn't scoff. She had seen him in action, knew that he could handle himself under the most trying conditions. Nevertheless, she felt it necessary to get in a final remark on the subject.

"You'd better be more than just ready, Deputy. That won't be enough—not near enough."

"We'll see," Luther murmured.

The day grew increasingly hot as they worked north-

ward across a vast mesa, gashed occasionally by deep arroyos and brush-filled washes, and low hills. Mountains
were beginning to take shape in the distance, a long,
gray-blue ragged mass that was miles in the offing. Capitol City lay somewhere near the range, Luther recalled,
and the penitentiary stood at the outskirts of the settlement.

They saw no one, very few living creatures at all, in
fact; a hawk soaring against the burnished sky, a curious
prairie dog that thrust himself partly out of his burrow to
observe their passage which went unnoticed by others in
the village; a lean coyote, fur matted, brush drooping as
he skulked through the false sage a safe distance from
them.

They were fortunate to make camp that night beside a
good spring, one that provided an acre-sized water hole
for some rancher's cattle, although none were to be seen
as they pulled up. Later that evening, near sundown, a
dozen or so lank steers drifted in, took their fill, and then
drew back to graze on the rich grass.

Once again at sunrise Luther had his prisoner up and
fed, and continuing the monotonous ride toward the hills
to the north. Both were weary, short on patience and
seething inwardly with angry frustration, although for
different reasons.

It was apparent that Nellie Dupray had expected help
long before this hour. It was likely she felt that her
friends, undoubtedly aware of the wrecking of the stagecoach and the course then taken by her captor, were at
fault for allowing her to be put through such a grueling,
uncomfortable journey at the hands of Luther Pike. She

could have been relieved of it all if those she was depending on were following instructions.

And Deputy Luther Pike. Most of the glitter had worn off the star he carried in his pocket, and he was coming to the inexorable conclusion that becoming a lawman was just another way to get involved in hard, back-breaking work—only with a different sort of danger to put up with.

A man riding the range, looking after cattle could find means a'plenty to get himself hurt—a horse stepping in a gopher hole, not being quick enough to dodge a rampaging steer, rattlesnakes that have a habit of lying in the same patch of shade a man decides to hunker down in— and a dozen or more other methods.

Wearing a badge out plain, going about doing what was expected of a lawman set him up as a target for every jasper with a price on his head, and some who didn't, that came down the trail.

Lawmen were marked, and it seemed to Luther that it wasn't only the outlaws and criminals he had to watch, but the ordinary, everyday folk as well. Nobody liked a man who wore a badge, he'd concluded; respected him, perhaps, were scared of him, maybe—but having a liking for him was not to be.

And that was the kind of life he'd chosen to embark upon—a genuine, bona-fide lawman; *had* embarked upon, in fact. Luther had puzzled over that while he and his prisoner worked steadily northward toward the completion of his first assignment. It wasn't at all like he'd figured it would be—endless hard work, worry, tension; going dry and hungry, making do with the barest of necessities and the crudest of facilities that even a cowhand out on the range wouldn't consider—and all the while waiting, keyed-up, for somebody to try and blow your head off. Hell, a man could get himself killed with a lot less sweat just punching cattle.

Being utterly honest about it, Luther was beginning to wonder if he really wanted to be a lawman—if he wouldn't like it better back with Percy Gilmore, and Arnie Payne, and Windy, and all the other cowhands on the range at Hockmeyer's, than putting himself through what he'd been undergoing ever since Sheriff Tom Hollingshead had pinned a badge on him. It seemed to him that he was in the same class as the man who kept hitting himself on the toe with a hammer—plenty dumb.

He was hashing that about, somewhat bitterly, in his mind when near noon, as they drew near a grove of trees, a dozen riders appeared, and spreading out into a wide half circle, came racing toward them.

Nellie's friends, at last! Luther swore. They had picked a good place to move in. Cutting him off from the grove as they were doing, there wasn't any place near where he could make a stand and fight, even with a pistol in each hand. But a sort of relief was coursing through Luther, regardless; the threat of friends Nellie had been beating him over the head with ever since Linksburg, had finally arrived.

The riders were quickly upon them, some swinging by at a dead run, to circle, close them in. Luther, realizing the futility of resistance, put away his weapons, and drew to a halt. Glancing at Nellie, he grinned wryly.

"Your friends outsmarted me after all, seems. I reckon the next move is up to you—and them."

Nellie, frowning, made no reply. Her pale gray eyes were on the leader of the party—a large, powerfully built, robust man with dark curly hair not only on his head but showing everywhere else on his muscular body not concealed by clothing. He had a square jaw partly covered by a short spade beard, and a heavy mouth over which curved a full mustache. Sawing savagely at the bit in his horse's teeth, he swung in near.

The animal was having a bad time of it. Bloody froth covered its muzzle, filled its nostrils, and its flanks were raw and running blood from the long-tined Mexican spurs its rider had used freely.

"It's them all right, Mr. Holt!" one of the riders sang out. "Both of them are wearing your brand."

"String the bastard up!" another shouted. "Get a rope—"

Alarm shot through Luther. These weren't Nellie's expected friends after all; this was some rancher named Holt, evidently, and a bunch of his cowhands—and they had him figured for a horse thief!

"Wait!" he shouted above the confusion of yells. "I'm a deputy sheriff! Never stole these horses, took them—"

"Sure you did!" a rider wheeling in alongside said and dropped a loop about Luther's shoulders. "I ain't never seen a horse thief yet that claimed he'd stole anything!"

"I didn't!" Luther shouted desperately. Sweat was standing out on his face in large beads as he frantically tried to get Holt's attention. "I'm a deputy—look in my pocket—papers there'll prove it!"

Holt was not listening. He had ridden in close to Nellie, was staring at her, an odd sort of grin cracking his thick lips.

"Nellie?" Luther heard the rancher say. "Ain't that you?"

The lawman, trying to squirm free of the rope that had tightened about his body and was pinning his arms to his sides, saw the woman nod.

"Sure is, Dave. Been a long time since Lordsburg."

"Holt!" Luther shouted the rancher's name with the loudest voice he could muster. "You got to listen to me! You're making a mistake—I ain't no horse thief, I'm a deputy sheriff!"

He watched the rancher turn to look at him, glimpsed his impassive features, saw him nod, and then in the next instant something crashed into the back of his head.

Lights popped in his brain, and a surge of pain accompanied by a sense of weakness overpowered him, caused him to buckle forward. Vaguely, as if from a great distance, a voice cried, "String up the bastard!"

✻ 18 ✻

Groggy, a dense, gray fog shrouding his brain, Luther became aware that he was being jerked about, of coming off his saddle and falling hard. The shock of striking solid ground jarred him to the bone, set things to spinning wildly inside his head.

"Get him up there—"

The speaker was next to him, yet the words seemed to come from far away. Hands seized him. The rope about his arms slackened briefly as he was boosted back onto a horse, grew taut once more.

"Them trees—over in the grove—"

Luther shook his head violently, struggled to throw off the paralysis that gripped him. He had no strength, could not make his muscles respond, nor could he focus his eyes.

"Hold on—wait!" he managed in a voice that sounded strangely unfamiliar.

"That big cottonwood—limb sticking straight out. Get that rope over it—put the noose around his neck."

He was going to be lynched! The fact drilled slowly into Luther's lethargic mind. They were going to string him up—and he wasn't guilty of anything—certainly not of stealing horses!

"No!" he croaked. "No—wasn't me!"

Mustering strength from somewhere, he stiffened, began to fight the hands clawing at him. A fist hammered at the side of his head. He sagged, recovered. He felt a rope on his shoulders, felt it slide up, become a noose around his neck. He tried to seize it, pull slack into the choking loop. Hands gripped his, jerked them behind his back, bound them roughly.

"I'm a deputy sheriff—a lawman!" he gasped. "You're making a bad mistake."

Luther's senses reeled as another blow caught him on the back of the head. He rocked forward, only slightly conscious of the milling horses, the shouting, the hanging dust—of a voice reaching through it all to him.

"Come on—let's get it over with!"

Lynched—strung up for a horse thief—him, a lawman, a deputy sheriff! Why the hell couldn't he make them listen? The thought, the question stumbled through Luther's reeling brain, sought to find an answer . . . if he could only get to that rancher, talk to him, make him see. The rancher—damn Nellie anyway—he was a friend of hers! Another friend! Seemed every man they ran into was. If she'd shut up, back off and get out of the way, maybe he'd have a chance to catch the rancher's attention, explain.

He realized the noose about his neck had loosened. The shouting had died and the confusion had tapered off. A moment later he heard the voice of Nellie Dupray.

"He's telling you straight—he's no horse thief."

"Then what are you and him doing riding a couple of my horses? Was stole right out of my corral—"

"He took them away from some deserters that jumped us night before last—I think it was. I don't know where they got them—from your corral, I guess—but they were heading west for California—so they claimed."

Holt, his dark face glistening with sweat, stared at the woman with half closed eyes. "Where was all this?"

"Below here—south, I guess it would be. There was a town not far from where we camped—was along a little stream."

"That'd be Anson, Mr. Holt," one of the riders volunteered.

The rancher stirred on the saddle. His horse, chewing constantly on the bit, fiddled nervously. "Yeh, reckon that's what it'd be."

Luther, totally conscious now, saw Holt's critical gaze turn to him. "He a deputy like he says he is?"

Fresh anger rolled through Luther. The rancher had heard him, yet had made no move to stop his men. If Nellie hadn't spoken up—

"Just what he is," he heard her reply. "Carries his star in his pocket. Can find his papers there, too, signed by the sheriff at Linksburg."

Holt, leaning forward, a forearm on the horn of his saddle, permitted his glance to take in Oglesby's two plow horses.

"I've seen some mighty sorry nags but that pair's about the sorriest. You'd be better off walking."

"Not the way we started out," Nellie said. "We were on the stage—going on business. Indians ambushed us, shot the driver. Coach turned over on a sharp bend in the road."

"Don't look like stage line horses to me—"

"They're not. They were taken by the Indians—the ones that weren't killed when we went off the road. We rented these from a homesteader we came to."

We! Luther looked more closely at the woman, struggling to understand. She was taking up for him now, actually protecting him. It was hardly the Nellie Dupray he knew—or thought he knew.

"Where was you headed?" Holt asked.

"North—"

"What for?"

"On business, like I said. I came along for the ride."

Holt raised a hand gestured at Luther. "Leave him go, boys. Them horse thieves we're after are down around Anson, seems."

Luther felt the noose being opened and slipped over his head. The rope that bound his wrists parted suddenly. He glanced to the rancher. Holt was leaning back on his saddle, an amused expression on his face as he considered Nellie.

"Well, I expect you've had about all the ride you want by now," he said, nodding to her. "My place is over the rise there, a piece behind us. You can come spend a few days—sort of lay around, do some resting up. I'll send my boys on south to deal with them horse-stealing deserters you was talking about."

Nellie shook her head, taking no time to think over the rancher's offer to become his guest. "Obliged to you, Dave, but I'll stick with my man."

"Man! Looks like some saddle tramp to me—"

"We've been riding, having it tough for the last few

days—ever since that coach turned over, in fact. Expect we both ain't much."

Holt rubbed at his jaw. "Plenty I can give you at my place, Nell—and you'll be welcome to stay long as you please."

Nellie frowned at the man's insistence, shrugged. "Like I said, Dave, I'm obliged, but that's not for me any more. I've settled down—and he's my husband. Maybe it ain't all honeysuckle and red roses—but it's what I want."

Holt's mouth tightened. "Your choice," he snapped, abruptly angry, and throwing a hard glance at Luther, jerked his horse about and spurred away from the grove.

For a moment the men with him were caught unready, even confused, and then one brushed at the sweat on his face.

"I reckon we all best head for Anson," he said, tiredly. "That's where he's going . . . Somebody bring along them horses."

Wheeling about, he struck off after the rancher. There was a bit of hesitation on the part of the others while one of their members took possession of the two horses belonging to Holt, and then all followed.

Luther, rubbing his chafed throat gingerly, watched the cowhands ride off and fade slowly into the shimmering heat waves. When they were no longer visible, he swung off the old broad-backed bay and retrieved his two pistols, half buried in the loose sand where they had been tossed.

Knocking the grit from each, and making certain both were in working order—and still puzzled by Nellie—he doubled back to his horse, pausing to pick up a short length of rope discarded by Holt's men, and climbed aboard.

Nellie, forced to change mounts, had already settled herself and was staring off into the distance—not in the direction taken by Holt and his riders, but north, toward the mountains, and Capitol City.

Luther, sweaty brow deeply furrowed, regarded her thoughtfully. Why had she lied for him?

✳ 19 ✳

Luther thumped his heels against the ribs of his horse, inducing him to start moving. Nellie's mount, without any encouragement from her, immediately swung in alongside, and the tedious journey began once more.

After they were underway Luther glanced at the woman. "You sure got me scratching my head! Just can't figure why you'd go to the trouble of saving my hide."

"Don't go getting ideas about it," Nellie said indifferently.

"Ain't—it's only that you could've shucked me, got me off your back, and gone on with that fellow, Holt."

"Yeh, guess I could."

"Time I could get word to the warden, or to some lawman, that you'd escaped, you could be in Mexico where nobody could touch you. That's what's chewing at me—why you didn't do that. Why'd you speak up like you did, saying all them lies for me?"

Nellie's mouth was a tight line as she turned to him. Her face was showing the burn of the sun, and her pantaloons, once white, were now a dusty gray with several dirt streaks.

"You got to have an answer to everything, Deputy?"

Luther mulled that about for a bit, finally nodded.

"Yes, guess I do. Just never was any hand to leave something fretting about in my head . . . You just had to keep your mouth shut back there and you'd been a free woman—"

"No need to keep reminding me."

"And telling him I was your husband—"

Nellie smiled wanly. "That did sort of cool old Dave down a bit, didn't it?"

"For certain. You know him long?"

"Too long," Nellie said flatly, the corners of her mouth pulling down. "From one night in Lordsburg."

"That all? Way it sounded to me you two were mighty good friends—"

"Nope, he's no friend of mine—not then, not now, and not ever! Maybe he'd like to think so, but it's all one sided far as I'm concerned. You want to know why I lied for you? Just this—anything would beat going with Dave Holt."

"Anything—I reckon that means me and the pen."

Nellie nodded. Luther wagged his head. "You sure must have something bad against him," he commented, and taking the canteen from the horn, pulled the cork and offered it to the woman. Nellie brushed it away.

"One night with him was enough," she said. "He's a hard man on women, same as he is on horses. Expect you saw how he treated the one he was riding."

Luther took a swallow of the tepid water, restored the cork and hung it back in place.

"Was something shameful," he said. "Them big Mex spurs was drawing blood like they was knives. Same with the bit. Horse's mouth was cut bad."

"He treats a woman the same way. After that night in Lordsburg I wasn't able to work for a week. Hell, Dave Holt ain't got enough money now, or ever will have enough to get me in the same room with him!"

"I see. Looked like his hired hands wasn't too crazy about him either. . . . Anyway, I'm sure obliged to you."

"No sense making over it," Nellie said. "My friends'll be coming along pretty soon. I'd been a fool to go off with Dave, or anybody else, when they're most likely close by."

"Reckon so," Luther murmured, "but I'm thanking you just the same."

He stirred uncomfortably, not from the driving heat or the slow, plodding gait of Oglesby's old horses, but at the feeling the woman's actions had awakened in him.

Regardless of what she had done for him, he could not allow himself to feel sorry for her, he cautioned himself. He was a lawman, top to bottom, and she was a prisoner who had been entrusted to him by his superiors—actually the court. He must let nothing get in the way of his sworn duty, which meant getting Nellie delivered to the territorial penitentiary.

But it was kind of a shame. A woman who would do what she did for him—her captor—couldn't be all bad. No matter what she had said about Dave Holt, and there had been real fear in her eyes when she spoke of the rancher, she could have let him go right ahead with the lynching, thus freeing herself of the man taking her to prison, and then getting away from Holt later. Nellie was a capable woman, accustomed to dealing with all sorts. If she had made up her mind that Dave Holt would never have her again, under any circumstances, odds were better than good that's the way it would be.

There was some good in her; what she had just done for him—speaking up with the truth, then lying, telling Holt and the others that he was her husband so that they would not harm him, proved that. And when you came right down to bare bone, Nellie should not be considered in the same light as those friends of hers that had been found guilty of rustling.

Actually, she was just a sort of helper. It was those friends who did the rustling—she only acted as a representative. You'd think that jury and the judge would have taken that into consideration before finding her guilty and sentencing her to spend the rest of her life behind bars.

It would have been a good thing if Nellie had grabbed her chance and gone along with Dave Holt. Getting roughed-up and manhandled certainly would be better than forevermore in the pen. Of course, he had no special yearning to have his neck stretched. His thoughts relative to what was best for Nellie were predicated on what she could have done after she had convinced the rancher that he was not a horse thief but had come into possession of the two horses innocently.

But it hadn't worked that way, and truth shining through all the murky ifs and ands like a pure, white light, labeled Nellie a criminal doomed—and rightly so—to live the remainder of her life in the pen; and that's all there was to it. No amount of telling himself it shouldn't be or feeling sorry for her could change the facts.

Anyway, he had sworn to uphold the law of the territory when he became a lawman, and he intended to do exactly that. It would be a hell of a note if, on his very first assignment as a deputy, he let the law down because he felt his prisoner, doing him a favor indirectly, didn't warrant the punishment that had been meted out.

Luther again swiped distractedly at the sweat on his stubbled face. This being a lawman was hard on a man's conscience! He sure hoped the next job Sheriff Tom Hollingshead sent him on was something simple, and not one that kept digging at him like this one did.

He glanced ahead, swept the flat, endless country with its lonely cedars visible here and there in the bright heat. No sign of riders—of Nellie's friends. He reckoned he'd better stop thrashing the whys and the why nots about in his head and keep a sharper lookout for them.

They were bound to show up, either yet that day or tomorrow, for it would be the final one. He grinned tightly . . . the end of the journey. He'd be shed of Nellie Dupray and all of the problems that went along with her—and that she'd brought down on him . . . Luther nodded in satisfaction; now he had his thinking straightened out, was looking at the situation as a good lawman should.

He had almost reached the point where he had considered turning the woman loose, freeing her, letting her go her way. But something had risen inside him, blocked it from his mind before he could actually give it thought. That was past now, all behind him; he was still a lawman and Nellie Dupray was still his prisoner—and would remain so until he handed her over to the warden.

Lifting an arm Luther shaded his eyes briefly with a

cupped hand, then pointed to a smear of dark green on the horizon.

"Looks like we're coming to some short hills," he said. "Expect there'll be a creek—along with trees and plenty of brush. We'll make camp there for the night."

Nellie turned, smiled at him. "All right, Deputy. Whatever you say."

There was a sadness in her tone, in the depths of her pale, gray eyes. Luther, immediately aware of it, frowned. And then a wry grin cracked his dry lips. Only minutes earlier he had felt sympathy for her and her plight. Now she was repaying in kind.

"You feeling sorry for me, ma'am?"

"I guess I am—"

"I reckon that means you're expecting your friends to show up real soon?"

"Could be, Deputy. Like to say now while I've got the chance that I'm obliged to you for treating me right. Told the sheriff that, and meant it. Goes double for you."

"Just part of my job," Luther said, and fell to watching the surrounding country more closely.

✖ 20 ✖

The broad mesa, covered with thin grass, spotted with yucca, snakeweed, occasional clumps of feathery Apache plume and gray-green rabbit brush seemed to run on indefinitely while the dark hills to the north seemed to draw no nearer.

It reminded Luther of the time he'd been on a cattle drive across the salt flats area of Texas, just north of the Mexican border. Hockmeyer had purchased a small herd from a rancher in the vicinity and he, along with Percy and a couple more of the hands had been sent to get the cattle and drive them back across the hundred miles or so of intervening country.

It was summer, August, Luther recalled, and the water holes had about all dried up, the sun was hotter than hell's fire, and the dust cloud hanging around the steers was thick as buttermilk. It was mean going and everyone was having a bad time of it, and all were hoping they'd pretty soon come to the ranch—but it never seemed to get any closer.

Tempers wore plenty short. Luther remembered two of the cowhands—Andy Queen and Curly Adams—got into a ruckus the third night out over something that neither of them, later, could rightly put his finger on. But when it was finished Luther remembered Curly standing off to the side near a big Mexican *canerjos* rubbing his jaw and saying he sure didn't intend to tangle with Andy ever again, that Andy'd hit him so hard his hair rattled.

It had been a tough, back-breaking, sweat-soaking job, but at night after the sun had gone down and they'd found a place to hold the cattle and make camp, things would ease off. They'd throw together a supper, which never varied from beans, beef, hardtack and black coffee, and after they'd eaten and the cattle were quiet, they'd sit around smoking and swapping lies while Arnie Payne played his jew's-harp. He was pretty good at it, actually, and every once in a while he'd come up with a tune a fellow could recognize and everybody would hush and listen, or maybe try singing along.

No matter how tired he might be, Luther remembered, he had always looked forward to those pleasant evenings —times when he maybe was so weary from the day's work that he could hardly move, but it was a good sort of tiredness. There was no big worry or responsibility plaguing him, and he had no problem getting to sleep.

All he had to think about was getting the herd through to the ranch and that called for nothing more than keeping an eye out for strays and lags, and not letting the dumb critters walk themselves into a dead-end canyon or get lost in the brakes.

Being a lawman was different. A fellow had to think of everything, be on the lookout for trouble from all sides, day and night—and bear up under responsibility heavy enough to bow the legs of an ox. Your friends all pulled away from you, more or less, and it was wise to be suspicious of everybody you met and be prepared to fight in the blink of an eye, if necessary.

Here he was, coming to the end of another day, one that had been filled with worry and tension, and the usual amount of just plain hard work. The night would be little different—more worry and tension that would last until sunrise—and then it would start all over again with the only difference being that it was daylight and not dark. It was an endless chain of stress, and as long as he wore a star, Luther was realizing, avoiding the trouble and grief that went with the job would be as impossible as running between raindrops.

Abruptly filled with wistfulness, he turned, looked back over his shoulder as if hoping for a glimpse of the life he had forsaken. Then, as quickly banishing the thought from his mind, he came back around, putting his attention ahead.

At last the flat land was breaking up. Smooth, round topped hills and low, red-and-gray-streaked bluffs began to appear. The shallow washes were becoming deeper, wider arroyos with glistening sandy floors. Gaunt cholla cactus, some with clusters of yellow blossoms, gathered in sparse groves, and on the slopes studded with rusty sandstone, prickly pear grew in disorderly beds.

They reached the first of the trees, a scatter of scrubby, pleasant smelling cedars and pinons thriving in a shallow coulee. Nellie glanced back at him questioningly. She was near exhaustion again, he knew, and he wished things might be easier for her, being a woman, but there was little he could do.

"Is this all right?" she asked.

Luther did not reply. A frown had drawn his features into taut lines. There was something wrong. He could sense it, almost feel it. Several times in the past such intuitive warnings had come to him, and he'd learned never to ignore them.

"Hold it a minute," he replied in a low voice, and slipping off his horse, he made his way quietly through the trees to the opposite side of the swale.

He drew up short. Five men, their mounts standing slack-hipped nearby, were hunched on their heels in the shade of the cedars. All were facing away from him—east. He threw his glance into the direction of their interest. Cutting through the rising slope was the main road that ran on to Capitol City.

Nellie's friends. . . . It came to him in a rush. They had pulled up there, a mile or so off the highway, watching and waiting for him to appear. Most likely they had been hanging around in the area for days.

Their original plan, if Nellie was to be believed, was to stop the north-bound stage somewhere along the way as it was passing through. The Indians had upset that scheme and they had been forced to ride on well ahead and wait, undoubtedly aware by that time that Nellie was being escorted not on a coach but either by a wagon or buggy, or on horseback—and by a remote trail.

Jaw set, eyes reflecting the seriousness of the problem that now faced him, Luther considered the surrounding country. The outlaws had chosen a good place to lay their ambush. The hills grew larger to both the east and west, and the road, following the easiest course, stayed low between them.

But the land was gathering to a central point, like a funnel, he saw, with the road continuing north to enter a sort of pass beyond which it probably again dropped down to a flat and wound on to the settlement at the foot of the distant mountains.

He could not get Nellie by the outlaws and make it to the pass without being seen, even under cover of darkness, Luther realized—and he wasn't fool enough to believe he could take on five men, all ready to shoot it out with him for the woman. He'd learned fast that the majesty of the law, as represented by a star, counted for nothing. Insofar as his authority as a deputy sheriff was concerned, among such men he might as well be a sheared sheep; his official standing intimidated nobody.

But perhaps there was a way. Maybe he wouldn't have to try getting past the outlaws with Nellie. The hills to either side were high, looked somewhat steep and rocky, and on their left were cluttered with brush. It could be he might find a trail of sorts that would take them to the crest, after which they could drop over on the yonder side without Nellie's friends being any the wiser.

Pivoting, he cut back to where he had left the woman and the horses, and swinging up onto the saddle, he pointed indefinitely off to their left.

"Best we keep going, leastwise for a while. It's a couple of hours yet 'til dark, and if we aim to make Capitol City tomorrow, we need to cover as much ground today as we can."

Nellie sighed, wiped at her face. "I don't know if I can go any farther—"

"Just set tight and hang on," Luther advised. "Your horse'll be doing all the work."

Taking a course that carried them away from the waiting outlaws, they began to climb at once. There was no trail, not even a faint one left by passing animals, and Luther, in the lead, picked the path as best he could.

For the first time since leaving Oglesby's he appreciated the horses they were riding. The big, heavily muscled plow animals, while moving with frustrating slowness, had the strength to ascend the grade and give no signs of tiring.

Near the summit of the hill, evidenced by a rocky hogback laying an irregular horizon against the darkening sky, Nellie called plaintively to him.

"Can't we stop—I—"

"Only a little piece to the top," he said, and let the bay continue.

Several times he studied the country to the east, eyes probing the brushy hollows and ragged bluffs for the outlaws, but the course he had chosen had evidently taken Nellie and him well to their west while still bearing gently north. When they finally gained the high-line crest of the hill and topped out, he had stopped searching for them, deciding that the men were now well behind them with their attention centered elsewhere, and he need not consider them a threat any longer.

"Them trees—down the slope a bit," he said, pointing. "We'll make camp there."

Nellie's answer was a long, thankful sigh. Then, "Mind telling me why we had to come clear around here, the hard way, when the road's down there on the flat?"

Luther could see no reason now why she shouldn't know. "Your friends—five of them—were waiting there in that first stand of cedars we came to. A couple of more minutes and we would've rode right into them. Swinging wide like we've done, we've given them the slip."

Nellie accepted the information with no change of expression. Then, shoulders stirring slightly, she said, "Sort of figured that's what was going on. . . . Looks like you're going to win, Deputy."

❈ 21 ❈

They made a dry camp in a coulee well within the cluster of trees—cedars, pinons and a pine or two. Despite the absence of a creek or spring to provide fresh water, it was a good place.

After halting Luther saw to the horses, loosening their saddle cinches, and slipping their bits, then swabbing their muzzles with a cloth wet from his canteen. Later, when they had cooled, he would again soak the rag but this time he would squeeze the cloth dry into their mouths.

The big, heavy-hoofed beasts had worked tirelessly in the heat and under trying conditions, and he wished he could do more for them. No doubt they were accustomed to hardship, but Luther still wished there was some way that he could reward them—some grain, fresh hay, perhaps. But it wasn't possible. Anyway, the journey would be over by that time next day, and he'd see that they received a bit of special attention.

Picketing them where they could graze on the grass available, Luther set about collecting dry wood that would create little smoke and odor while burning. Nellie, worn and spiritless, made no effort to help. Sitting on a rock, shoulders against the trunk of a pine, she watched him get the meal together, and when it was ready, ate her portion in the same, sullen manner.

Later, when they had finished and Luther had built up the small fire to some extent—no longer fearing that its smoke might be seen, Nellie seemed to come to life.

Taking her handkerchief she wet it from her canteen and proceeded to clean her face, neck, hands and arms. Then, working with her hair, and with the help of her scarf, she restored it to some semblance of order. Satisfied with what she had accomplished on that score, she put her attention on her dress, releasing it from where it was knotted and tucked about her waist and allowing it to fall and conceal her pantaloons, now a dust and dirt-streaked gray.

He'd be more than happy to rid himself of Nellie Dupray, Luther had to admit. The job of escorting her to prison had been far from what he'd expected, and his thoughts kept returning to his previous, carefree and easy-by-comparison way of life at Hockmeyer's ranch. The worst side of punching cattle was a snap when you lined it up against being a lawman.

Maybe a man could feel a bit more satisfaction in working for the law than he could in chasing cows out of the brush, but on the other hand—maybe pride wasn't all that important! It could be a man was meant to live his life at an easy stride, taking time to be aware of all the fine things like smelling the flowers and marveling at the tall trees and having a longer look at the sun's rising and setting, and such, and not be so bound to a job and weighted with responsibility that he missed such miracles.

Some men, he reckoned, were cut out to be the responsibility-bearing kind; it was their nature and he supposed they got fat and sassy on it, but he was wondering now if they didn't steal a few minutes occasionally to stop, look back longingly at what they'd missed—and maybe wished they hadn't.

It seemed to him it would be mighty hard to ignore the world around him—all that blue sky filled sometimes with great masses of swirling cotton floating majestically across it, other times dark with banks of thick, surly-looking clouds racing for the horizon; the towering hills, the endless flats gashed by arroyos, the clear, clean streams, the wild things that roamed freely over it all.

Well, he'd not lose touch no matter what sort of job his career as a lawman required him to undertake, Luther vowed silently, and then frowned. He'd covered a good many miles of new country during those last few days, and coming to think about it, he'd been so busy looking after Nellie and keeping them both alive, he hadn't taken time to see much of anything—let alone smell the daisies.

He swore quietly, shook his head. Already he was lapsing into that state of blindness, induced by responsibility, wherein he was aware of his surroundings but actually saw none of it. Ordinarily, if he had been passing through pushing a herd of cattle to some certain point, or just loafing along on an errand, he would have taken in the land, noted the grass, the trees and brush that were common to the area, the hills, rocky formations, creeks and all else that made up a new country. This time he—

"Deputy—"

At Nellie's voice Luther came from the depths of his troubled thoughts, glanced across the low fire at her.

"Yes, ma'am?"

She smiled at him, moved slightly from side to side in order that he might have a better look at the results of her preening.

"Do I look any better?" she asked, circling the fire and sitting down beside him.

"Reckon so," Luther replied. "Sure am sorry there wasn't no creek we could've stopped by."

"Doesn't bother me if it doesn't bother you," she said, flippantly. "You know, I'm not the least bit sorry you dodged those friends of mine."

Luther frowned, scratched at the stubble on his jaw. "Ain't sure I know what you mean—"

"Down deep I don't want you to get hurt—maybe even killed."

He grinned. "Obliged to you for feeling that way, but I reckon I can look out for myself. Been doing it for a good many years now."

"But there're five of them—all hard cases and gunmen!"

"Figured that's how it'd be. A fellow has to look at his hole card at a time like that, come up with something that'll help him better the odds."

"Well, thank goodness you won't need to worry about that now," Nellie said, smoothing the folds of her dress in her lap. "We'll be reaching Capitol City tomorrow sometime, I expect."

Luther nodded. Now and then Nellie talked like a schoolteacher, other times she sounded like a saloon girl. Whatever education she'd gotten as a preacher's daughter couldn't help showing through every once in a while, he guessed.

"Not for sure, but I figure we'll make it in the afternoon—late."

"I see . . . Luther, I've been wondering—"

He was a bit surprised at her calling him by his first name. Half smiling, he said, "Yeh?"

"About us. I've grown real fond of you—us being together the way we have these last few days—the danger, trouble and the like. Has it meant anything to you?"

Luther pulled off his hat, ran splayed fingers through his shock of thick hair, allowed his hand to slide on down and explore the bristle on his cheeks.

"I—I ain't sure I know what you're getting at," he said, haltingly.

"I'm asking if I've come to mean anything to you? You have to me."

He continued to rub at the stubble, all the while staring into the fire. "I ain't allowed to have any feelings like that toward a prisoner," he said, finally. "Wouldn't be right. I took an oath—"

"Forget that!" Nellie cut in, turning to him. "Forget all about the job you got pushed off on you, and team up with me. We can head east or west—or any direction that suits you, and keep going 'til we hit a town. I can get a job, make money anywhere I go—plenty to support both of us."

The weather-browned planes of Luther Pike's face had tightened and his eyes had spread slightly. "You saying for me to just forget about taking you to the warden, and the pair of us riding on, going somewheres and living like man and wife?"

"That's exactly what I mean, Luther! We could have us

a good life together—do some traveling around, see all the big towns like New Orleans and Dallas and San Francisco —where the ocean is."

"I ain't much in favor of letting a woman support me," he said slowly, "but it sure sounds inviting. What about them friends of yours? Won't they come looking for us?"

"Maybe—but chances are they'd never find us."

"I'm not so sure. We ain't going nowhere very fast on these old plugs we're riding. Your friends could catch us on foot if they tried."

"You get me to Denver and I'll buy us two of the best horses that can be had!" Nellie said, rushing her words, and then, catching herself, settled back. "Just you get me to Denver, like I've said. You won't ever have cause to regret it."

Luther made a final scrub of his chin, wagged his head. "I reckon I'd best do some apologizing to you, ma'am, for causing you to say all them things. Somewhere along the line I must've given you the idea that I was for sale. Well, now, maybe I ain't much on looks, or any kind of a big lawman, but I sure ain't what you're trying to make me out to be!"

Nellie laid her hand on his arm, smiled. "I'm sorry, Luther," she said, contritely. "I didn't mean it the way you're taking it. I just thought—if I'd come to be as important to you in these past days as you have to me, why we should—"

"Nope," Luther broke in bluntly. "I'm obliged, but I couldn't do nothing like that. You're a mighty fine looker of a woman, one I'd be proud to be seen with—"

"And call your own?"

"Yes'm, call my own, but I couldn't ever look myself in the eye again was I to do something like that."

"Even if it not only meant a lot of money to you—besides me?"

He frowned, again scratched at his jaw. Raising his head, he stared off into the blackness of the night. From somewhere back of them in the hills a wolf sent up a tremulous challenge that went unanswered.

"If you don't want me—" Nellie said, hesitantly, "I—"

"Ain't so much the wanting or not wanting, it's just that it wouldn't be right—or honest."

Nellie's shoulders stirred indifferently. She leaned forward, picked up a handful of branches and tossed them onto the fire.

"You've got to change your thinking, Deputy," she said, "if you're going to get anywhere in this life. Rules are for suckers to follow—and you're no sucker, I've found that out. You're rock-bottom smart, and you could go a far piece if you'd forget about whether something is wrong or right, and grab things as they came to you."

"That how you and your friends look at it?"

"It is, and—"

"Seems to me it ain't working so good for you, being on the way to the pen like you are. And them friends of yours, I expect the law'd like to get its hands on them, too."

Nellie considered him for a few long minutes, and then sighed deeply. "I just can't make you understand. Let me make it plain—straight-out talk. You take me to Denver and I'll pay you five hundred dollars in gold."

"Five hundred—in gold," he echoed in a lost sort of

voice. "And all I have to do is forget my job and get you to Denver?"

"That's all—"

Luther's gaze was lost in the flickering fire. Back in the hills the wolf howled again, once more failed to arouse an answer.

"You agree, we'll celebrate tonight! The two of us will have us a high old time."

"Well, that's sure a lot of money—more'n I've ever seen," Luther said finally, "and I ain't so pure that spending a night on a blanket with you wouldn't be real fine—but I reckon I'll have to pass. Just couldn't live with myself if I ever done something like that."

Nellie jerked away impatiently, got to her feet. Moving around to where she was opposite him she halted, glanced back. The glow of the flames mirrored the anger in her eyes.

"You're a damn fool, Deputy—the stupidest kind of a fool! I'm offering you a chance most any man I've ever met would jump at."

"I guess I just ain't any man," Luther said dryly, adding more wood to the fire.

"No, that's certain, but there's something you will be for sure by this time tomorrow."

He glanced up. "Yeh? What?"

"Dead," Nellie said flatly. "You won't get by my friends. They'll find us, and when they do—"

"You best be getting some sleep," Luther cut in quietly. "I aim to get an early start in the morning. G'night."

Nellie swept him with a withering look, and taking up her blanket, selected a place beyond the flare of firelight and settled down for the night.

22

A feeling of impending trouble and danger was again nagging at Luther. They had gotten away from the camp in the trees shortly before dawn; he had been anxious to prepare the morning meal early so that any smoke from the fire would not be seen.

That precaution had gone for nothing, he now feared. Not long after they had ridden out he glanced back, saw a column of thick, dark smoke winding up from the grove. Turning angrily to Nellie, he saw that she was smiling.

"You threw some green branches on that fire when I wasn't looking—"

Her smile had widened. "I've been telling you all along that you're playing a losing hand, Deputy. My friends will see that smoke and head this way in a hurry. They'll figure it's us."

"Yeh, I expect they will," Luther had agreed, wearily, putting his attention to probing the country for signs of the outlaws.

That had been hours ago, and now, late in the morning, as they slowly drew abreast the first high mountain, Luther was stirring restlessly on his saddle, eyes whipping back and forth constantly as he searched for the fulfillment of his hunch.

It materialized shortly after they reached the rocky, brush-littered slope of the towering formation. Five men, moving in fast, appeared suddenly. They were coming from the south—the direction of the grove. Nellie's trick had apparently worked. They had spotted the slender, dark line twisting up into the sky, and had hurried to investigate. Somewhere along the way they had caught sight of two riders, guessed correctly their identities, and set out at once in pursuit.

Nellie, dabbing at her face with a handkerchief, studied Luther slyly. After a bit she said, "You might as well pull up, Deputy, make it easy on all of us."

He was glancing about, raking his brain for an idea, a plan. It was clear—he had but two options: run for it, or stand and fight. There was no possibility of outdistancing the outlaws on Oglesby's plow horses, so he had no choice but the latter.

"No, I reckon not," Luther said, and pointed to a ragged mound of rocks and brush about halfway up the slope. "Start climbing. I aim to fort-up there."

Nellie stared at him, threw a quick look at her friends, now less than a mile away. She shook her head.

"No—I'm not moving—"

Luther swore vividly and drew out his handcuffs. "I ain't got the time to mess with you, lady! Them friends of yours means business, and I for sure don't figure to accommodate them on their terms. Either you head up the slope, or I'm cuffing you to your stirrup and letting your horse drag you all the way. Just make up your mind which real quick!"

Nellie muttered something under her breath, considered briefly the consequences of being towed up the rough surface of the hillside by her horse, or climbing it on her own, and nodded.

"All right—but it's a waste of time. You don't stand a chance."

"Man can't do nothing more'n try," Luther said. Dropping from the saddle, he took the reins of his horse and started the ascent, pausing long enough to see that the woman did likewise.

Breathless, sweat-soaked, they reached the rocks. The horses had fared badly, both going to their knees several times, but on each occasion Luther had pulled them back up and they had stubbornly continued.

The mound was more suitable than Luther had hoped it would be. At some time in centuries past a mighty upheaval had shaken the earth, creating the mountain and leaving a thick ledge of granite protruding from its side. During the passage of ensuing time winds had filled the crevices, brush had taken root and grown, and boulders, loosened by wild storms lashing the higher regions of the formation, had rolled down to lodge against the shelf and form a sort of rampart that overlooked the land below.

Hurriedly leading the horses as far back on the ledge as possible and tying them to one of the squat shrubs, Luther returned to Nellie. She was standing at the edge of the mound watching her friends. Their approach had slowed and they were looking up at the ledge uncertainly as they drew near the foot of the slope.

"Best you set yourself down behind one of them big rocks," he said, drawing his pistol and checking its loads.

"There's going to be shooting and one of them friends of yours just might hit you—accidental, of course."

Nellie made no reply. Grim faced, beads of sweat standing out on her forehead and upper lip, still breathing hard from the climb, she turned, crossed to the center of the ledge and sat down in a shallow depression next to a large rock.

Luther nodded approval, and then added, "I just want for you to know that if you try taking a hand—like maybe hitting me on the head with something—I'll have to shoot you. Now, if you figure you're apt to be tempted, I can handcuff you to one of them bushes—"

Nellie shook her head and looked away. Luther smiled and resumed checking his weapons. His own pistol was ready, and dropping it into its holster, he drew McGee's from his belt and examined it. There were two spent cartridges, four that were live. He swore softly. He'd get but four shots from it, and that was all; it was a different caliber from his gun.

Deciding he was set, Luther pivoted, and crouched low, made his way to the center of the rocks. It was like walking into an oven, and each time he laid his hand on one of the blistering hot boulders to steady himself, he cursed, jerking away. But finally he reached a place where he could look down and see the entire slope below and still be protected by the rim of the formation.

The outlaws had pulled to a stop at the foot of the hill, dismounted and were talking among themselves. Shortly they separated, two moving out to either side, obviously planning to come at him from opposite sides once they gained the level of the shelf. The others, stringing out like a forage line, started directly up the grade.

Luther watched them narrowly as they came on, each taking advantage of the boulders that had missed the ledge and tumbled farther down the hillside, and the patches of thick brush that could hide a man from view but furnish little protection from a bullet.

They were all still well beyond pistol range, and Luther had a quick regret that he didn't have his rifle with him— an old but reliable forty-four Remington. It was back in Linksburg with his horse and the rest of his gear. At that moment it sure would come in handy; he could pick the outlaws off one by one—easy as shooting fish in a water bucket.

"You—up there—Pike!"

Luther came up sharply. The voice was familiar. Pulling off his hat, he peered over the edge of the granite bulwark behind which he crouched and took a quick survey. The three men advancing up the slope had halted, each behind a different rock. The pair tediously working a course to each side of him were keeping at a safe distance and still had a ways to go before coming into the reach of his pistols.

"Who are you?" he shouted.

"Pete Peabody," the answer came. "The deputy you—"

Surprised, Luther didn't wait for the rest of the man's reply, but swung his shocked glance to Nellie. She smiled in a sly, confident manner.

"I told you before that you couldn't win, Deputy. Better listen to him."

Luther, frowning, shook his head. "Sure don't savvy this —him being a lawman and—"

"Pete's a sort of a partner of mine," Nellie said. "We worked together right along—him keeping me posted on what the law was doing so's I could always be somewheres else when one of Hollingshead's posses had a trap all laid for me and the boys."

"But you got caught, anyhow," Luther said, woodenly.

"That wasn't Pete's fault. There was a slip-up and he tried to get word to me, but he didn't make it."

"Sure hard to believe—him being a deputy—"

"Money—that's what makes the difference. Big reason him and those other men are here now. I've got a pile of cash salted away—cash me, Farr, Grubbs and Potts made before the rope caught up with them and I got jailed.

"I told Pete while I was locked up that I'd split it down the middle with him and the rest of the boys that was working with us, if they'd see to it that I never got taken to the pen. That's what they're doing right now—stopping you."

"Pike!" It was Peabody again. "We're giving you a chance to back off. Let Nellie come down here to us and we'll pull out and leave you be."

"No," Luther called back.

"Better think it over—you're buying yourself a grave."

"Maybe, but there'll be a couple of you laying right alongside me," Luther said. "From where I'm setting I can sure have an easy time picking you off."

"Not with the odds all against you—"

"That ain't nothing new. Been that way from the start —from when we left Linksburg. But you're figuring wrong. Odds've changed. It's me setting in the driver's seat now."

"You're looney!" Nellie said in a tone filled with disbelief. "You can't stand up against all five of them! They'll come at you from all sides—fill you so full of holes you'll—"

"I ain't planning on it," Luther drawled, both guns out and ready. "Best you yell down there to your friends, tell them I ain't fooling. I sure don't want to kill nobody, but I ain't turning you over to them, either, so what they ought to be doing is forgetting us, and going on about their business."

Nellie shrugged, brushed at the sweat on her face, partly shrouded by the scarf. "I guess you could say this is their business—taking me away from you."

A gunshot crackled in the still, hot air. Chips flew from a rock a short distance to Luther's right, and the glancing bullet went screeching off into space. Ducking instinctively, he shook his head.

"Well, I reckon the time's come," he said, and again peering over the edge of the boulder in front of him, he located one of the outlaws. Resting his pistol on the rock's hot, solid surface, he took aim and pressed off a shot. The man rose suddenly, threw out his arms and fell backward down the slope.

"That there's number one!" he shouted to the men on the hillside. "Next fellow to take a step toward me'll be number two—so keep coming! Hell ain't but one step ahead of you!"

Motion to his left caught Luther's eye. Keeping low, he pivoted to face that direction. The outlaw who had been circling in on him from that side of the slope was running across a strip of open ground and coming directly toward him. Bringing up his pistol swiftly, Luther snapped a bullet at the hurrying figure. The outlaw paused in stride, lurched, and went rolling down the grade in a cloud of dust.

"Who was that?" a voice called.

"The kid—Billy," someone replied. "He's plugged Yuma, too." There was a few moments silence and then the same voice continued, "I ain't so sure about this, Pete."

"Keep your shirt on," Peabody said. "We'll get to him . . . Nellie, you all right?"

"She's all right," Luther answered. "I'll be handing her over to the warden this afternoon."

"Like hell you will!" Peabody shouted. "Come on—let's rush him!"

Luther swung his attention to the right. The outlaw who had been working his way in from that side should be getting within range. Surprise rippled through him. The man, almost on a level with the ledge, and not too far off, had turned and was starting back down the slope. It would be easy to drop him, but there was no need. He was quitting.

"Joe—what the hell're you doing?" It was Peabody. He had caught sight of the outlaw's unexpected change, also. "Start cutting across—like we planned."

Joe maintained his descent, making no sign of having heard. Peabody began to curse him, and then abruptly stepped out from behind the rock where he had halted.

"Come on, Park!" he shouted to the one remaining man

on the hillside, and began firing his weapon at the rocks where Luther was crouching. "One of us is bound to hit him!"

Luther, eyes narrowed against the glare, leveled his weapon at the one-time deputy. Smoke was hanging on the slope, mixing with the dust stirred up by the outlaw's scuffing boots, and the echo of gunshots was almost a steady roll.

"Hold it—right there!" he warned, raising his voice to be heard. "Don't want to shoot you, but I'll sure have to unless you quit!"

Park hesitated and lowered his pistol, recognizing the futility of charging up the slope in the face of Luther's deadly aim. Peabody seemed neither to hear Luther nor notice that his partner was dropping out. He emptied his weapon, jerked another from his belt and came on.

Luther brushed sweat from his eyes, sighing resignedly. Ignoring the crack and snarl of bullets striking the rocks about him, he steadied his hand on the hot granite surface, drew a bead on Peabody's weaving shape, and triggered his pistol.

Pete Peabody halted, threw back his head. A piercing scream burst from his flared mouth, one that sent chills racing up Luther's spine and roused echoes all the way to the top of the mountain. And then he toppled, and like the others before him, went tumbling in a swirl of dust to the foot of the slope.

Suddenly overwhelmed and sick, Luther turned away, and leaning on the boulders oblivious to their stored, intense heat, rid himself of his morning meal. That done, he swung his attention back to the flat rolling out from the base of the mountain.

Park had mounted his horse and was racing to overtake the man called Joe, already moving south at a steady lope. A decision swept Luther abruptly, and determined to get the job over with as soon as possible, once and for all, he wheeled. Sweat streaming off his gaunt face, sodden clothing clinging to his weary frame, he moved out of the rocks and beckoned impatiently to Nellie.

"Let's go," he said, starting toward the horses. "I aim to get you handed over to that warden before dark."

⚔ 23 ⚔

Slope, the warden at the penitentiary, had been surprised to see Luther when he rode through the gate with Nellie Dupray.

"We'd about given you up," he'd said. "Figured them Indians that's on the warpath down your way—or maybe some of Nellie's friends—had got you."

"They all tried a'plenty," Luther admitted, and made a brief explanation.

Then, after completing the necessary work, and favored by no farewell from Nellie, he returned to Capitol City where he treated himself to a good meal, spent the night, and at the first sign of dawn, headed south.

He'd gone directly to homesteader Oglesby's place, managing to get in close enough to talk before the irate farmer could make use of his shotgun. He handed over all but five dollars of the expense money the sheriff had provided him with as part payment for rental of the two old horses, and after promising more would be forthcoming once he reached Linksburg, persuaded the man to take him to the nearest way station where he could catch the stage west.

Now, with the sun dropping low and the shadows of Linksburg's buildings stretching out across the dusty street, Luther, the lone passenger in the coach, sat hunched forward on the seat watching the structures glide by as the vehicle rolled swiftly up to the hotel.

It had hardly stopped when he was out of the door and on the board sidewalk. He stood for several moments looking off into the golden haze of dusk, and then features set, he strode briskly to the office of Tom Hollingshead.

The sheriff was alone, sitting at his desk, as Luther entered. He glanced up, smiled, rocked back in his chair.

"I'm mighty proud of you, Deputy!" he boomed, pointing to a letter lying before him. "This came in on the stage yesterday. From Warden Slope. Told me what'd happened—how you'd got the woman delivered to him in spite of everything. Hell about Peabody. Sure never suspected him of being in with her and her bunch."

Luther took it all with no change of expression. Back in the jail a prisoner was rattling the door of his cell for some reason, and over at the church, a few yards to the rear of the structure housing the law, choir practice was underway.

"But it's all done with now," Hollingshead said, "and like I've told you, it was a good job. Now, I hate to rush things, but there's work to be done. Soon as you get yourself cleaned up and buy some new duds, I want you to—"

"Sheriff—"

"Ride over to—"

"I'm quitting, Sheriff—"

Hollingshead's voice broke off abruptly. He stared at Luther, the folds of his neck bunched and overflowing the collar of his shirt.

"How's that?"

I

"Said I was quitting," Luther repeated, dropping his star and letter of authority on the lawman's desk.

Hollingshead, puzzled, fingered the star. "Thought you wanted to be a lawman—make a career of it, like me. And after the fine job you've done—which proves you'd make a real good lawman—I can't quite figure you out. Why'd you go through with it when you started running into all that trouble? You could've just said the hell with it, and walked off."

"Gave you my word I'd deliver the prisoner. Sure couldn't go back on it."

The sheriff rubbed at his jaw. "You're making a mistake—"

Luther glanced out the window, his thoughts on Percy Gilmore and Windy and all the other hired hands at Hockmeyer's. It would be good to get back and start working with them again. Of course, he could figure on taking a lot of guying, but he could stand it because he knew now where he belonged—punching cows. He guessed he wasn't cut out to be a lawman after all, like Percy had predicted—and since a man lived only once it was common sense to spend that life doing what he liked best.

"No, I reckon not," he said. "I owe you anything?"

"Expect it's the other way around," Hollingshead replied. "I probably owe you a couple of dollars."

Luther nodded, turned for the door. He was anxious to get his horse and gear, reach Hockmeyer's before all the supper grub was gone.

"Just forget it, Sheriff," he said. "I sure aim to—along with everything else about being a lawman."